NORTHERN V

An anthology of short stories, poems and screenplay
by Creative Writing Honours year students at the
University of the Highlands and Islands

Edited By

Kirstie Gunn

Table of Contents

Acknowledgments

We'd like to give a huge thanks to Caithness businesses Queen's Hotel of Wick, Simpson Oils, and Kat Mackenzie of Kat's Kups 'n' Kakes/ Kat's Kaithness Tipple, who kindly sponsored us for the publication of this project. We'd also like to give a special thanks to Ashleigh Tucker as our key fundraiser, and to S.J. Milne for her hard work designing the front and back cover. The proceeds of this anthology are going to The Leanne Trust, supporting people with Cystic Fibrosis across the north of Scotland.

Queen's Hotel

About the Author(s)

This collection was written by Honours year students on the BA Creative Writing in the Highlands and Islands degree at the University of the Highlands and Islands as a part of one of their final projects. We come from many different social and geographical backgrounds, though most of us are now based within the Highlands of Scotland.

Introduction

Kirstie Gunn

As part of one of their final Honours year modules, this group of writers was tasked with creating an anthology publication showcasing their work. The academic side of this involved me, as their Semester 2 tutor and newly appointed Programme Leader for BA Creative Writing in the Highlands and Islands at the University of the Highlands and Islands, as well as their Semester 1 tutor Sara Bailey, guiding them through the difficult process of the writing of the pieces, piece selection and ordering, workshopping and then the close editing of individual pieces and the anthology as a whole, and, of course, marking their final assessments.

But it has been so much more than that.

I first taught this wonderful group of students when they entered their first year on the degree in 2019. At this point, I was just starting out in my teaching career, and I was nervous and absolutely suffering from 'impostor syndrome,' but as this group has grown in confidence as writers, I have grown along with them, both in my career and in my own writing journey. We have worked as a close-knit team and a supportive community of authors, comforted each other through deadline stresses and crises in writing confidence, and, most of all, laughed and shared adventures together (both in real life and the virtual world). I am overjoyed to be able to say that they are now not just my students but my friends. I could not have asked for a more talented, wonderful, funny, and dedicated group of students to work with. We have gone through the many troubles that the pandemic brought us both personally and professionally together, persevered despite it all, and I am truly thankful for having had this experience with them.

During the module, as we put our anthology together, we discussed what its overarching 'theme' should be. The idea was that they could then rewrite or edit existing pieces to cater to that theme, but what we discovered was that, quite naturally, almost all of the writers had written pieces with some type of journey – spiritual, emotional, or physical – at their core. I am so glad that this theme came to fruition so easily, and I believe it is because we really have been on a journey together, which has organically fed itself into their writing. I hope that this is reflected in the pieces that follow. These pieces really do showcase the best of their work and how talented they all truly are, and I hope that anyone reading will sit up and take notice of their names because they have bright futures – as bright as the Northern Lights that inspired the (much debated over!) anthology title. Most of all, though, I hope that you, the reader, will find delight in reading this collection and perhaps shed a tear because I can vouch for how hard they have all worked on putting it together. It hasn't always been easy, but no journey worth undertaking ever is. They deserve all the praise I am sure that they will get for it.

Mother in Waiting

Robyn Kerr

Crying in the car.

Still no blue line,

empty.

It hasn't happened,

again.

I had let my hope take over;

lists of names on paper,

colour schemes in my head,

dreams of a baby reveal.

Is it me?

Something I've done wrong?

But I do as asked.

Take the pills by the dozen,

tests in the hundred,

injections I withstand,

supplements I endure.

I have done it all,

not only once.

A first,

then second,

a third,

then a fourth.

Now onto the fifth.

Virology, collecting, freezing;

how many embryos have made it this time?

Side effects becoming my norm,

bleeding, pain, bruising,

bloating, cramping.

Torn down,

fallen apart.

How many times can I go through it?

A wish I hold,

love to give.

When will the time come?

When will someone call me mum?

During my third year of university, I was placed in a research lab that dealt with IVF treatment. I was extremely moved and inspired by the couples yearning to become parents but finding the process devastating. Looking into the process and everything that it involves, I found myself creating this piece, Mother in Waiting, a powerful and emotional poem showing the pain of a mother without a child.

Friends and Foes

Catherine Halliday

Katie and I arrived at the church too early. I was forty minutes early – Katie was forty years. I didn't trust the Sat Nav when it told me that it would take twenty minutes to travel across Inverness in the rush hour. It didn't – it took far less.

Katie took a tumble off a mountain. One careless moment and she was gone. Forever. She was only forty-four, fit and healthy.

The church car park was quiet, with only my hire and one other car. The church itself was firmly closed. The large wooden door still showed traces of its once rich blue in the corners where the sun hadn't reached. Slightly concerned that I had the details wrong, I got out of the car to check the noticeboard. The wind had a cold nip to it, but it was fresh and clean. It was so unlike the polluted London that I'd left last night. I took a moment just to breathe it in. It was also quiet. No, not quite, I could hear little birds flitting around the bushes. Tranquil.

Katie Bruce (nee MacMillan), funeral Kirkhill church, 10 September 2022, 11 am. There it was in black and white. My bright, bubbly, beautiful best friend was dead. I tried to picture her as the wild lassie with whom I'd misspent my youth, but instead, what came to mind was the subdued Katie who'd visited me last summer. Her skin still shone, and her hair, now a tame bob than the tousled curls, the rich color of autumn, but her sparkle had dimmed. She'd been quiet and distracted. I'd put it down to us finally growing up – becoming respectable married ladies. Although that said, I am a slightly irresponsible divorced lady. Who would have guessed when they knew us as twenty-somethings in London in the 1980s that it would be me, twice married and divorced, and Katie who'd be the one to marry a surgeon and settle in a remote part of the Highlands?

The church was situated on a little hill, and I wandered around its exterior, admiring the view it gave across green fields and the Beauly

Firth to heather-clad hills in the distance and taller Munros further yet. It was a beautiful spot, rich in colour, unlike my city home, and in other circumstances, it would have raised my spirits.

Cars were starting to pull up. Feeling self-conscious, I hopped back into my car to check my emails. It was just the usual – writers wishing me to chase publishers about their manuscripts and publishers chasing other writers for their over-due manuscripts. Nothing that the staff back in London couldn't handle. I read the BBC headlines and then switched the phone off. Today was about Katie.

When the funeral cars pulled up, I joined the small crowd waiting to go in. I didn't recognise anyone. I had thought that there might be some school friends there – Inverness wasn't so far from Edinburgh, and I was sure Katie had kept in touch. She was good that way. The cars emptied, and we all took a step backward towards the shelter of the wall as if deep sorrow were infectious and not just awkward.

Rob, a blood-red rose clutched in his hand, kept his eyes firmly on the wicker coffin which was carried unsteadily ahead of him. I hadn't seen him for a long time and was surprised by how hunched, broken, and much older he looked. I had never really taken to him, but my heart went out to him at that moment. Katie had been his life. They had been such an item – the dream couple.

I hung back until all those waiting outside entered the building before following in. Inside was barely warmer than outside, and the air had that musty airless smell that seems unique to churches everywhere. It had been years since I had been in a Scottish church, and I had forgotten how beautiful its plain, simple interior was, especially after the Church of England's grand, ornate style. The back rows were already full, allowing their occupants a front-row seat on the catwalk of those coming in. I'd no idea who they were, neighbours, friends? She hadn't mentioned many friends to me, but then we'd not been so close lately. My heels clacked loudly on the stone floor as I made my way down the aisle. I felt all eyes on me, a stranger in their midst. The few family mourners in the front row turned to see who was making

7

such a noise. I instinctively smiled at Rob, who acknowledged me with a curt nod but quickly turned away. I dropped my smile and stared at the floor, feeling stupid for being so crass.

I turned in at the next row. It was about six from the front, which I felt was where I fit in Katie's life. I had met her aged six when she'd sat next to me in primary school and had made me laugh, and almost forty years later, she could still make me laugh. I had known her longer than almost everyone in the building, including her husband. There's a certain bond when you grow up with someone and share experiences - when you know their parents and family before you or their siblings know yourself. It's an unbreakable bond, almost like a family. My mother worked, which was unusual in Edinburgh in the 1980s, and rather than go home to a cold, empty house, I would go to Katie's. Her mother was the gentlest of souls and always made me feel welcome, even when, at times, during the ups and downs of childhood friendships, Katie didn't. I spent half my primary school days there.

Katie's bright smile stared at me from the back of the order of service. It was a lovely photograph of her and Rob - he had his arm around her. It had obviously been taken on top of a mountain. I guessed abroad, given the bright blue sky and snow, but I couldn't help thinking it was a bit indelicate given the manner of her death. It wasn't like she was a mountaineer – she did a bit of hillwalking but only in the summer. The inside photograph was of Rob and Katie on their wedding day. She looked so happy. Yet, I wished he'd picked one photo of just Katie. It seems her life was fated to be wrapped up with Rob's, even in death.

I sat in the middle of the row, leaving room on either side, but nobody joined me. That, too, felt appropriate – a rebuke for having barely been in Katie's life for the last five years. It wasn't as if I hadn't tried. When she first moved north, she came down to London regularly and was the wild, mad party Katie that we knew and loved. But as time passed, our shared friends grew away, and we all moved on in our lives and careers. Well, if I am honest, my career took off but also took over. Katie's visits got fewer and fewer until that last time a year ago when we seemed as strangers. I went to Inverness a few times to see her over the years, but I always felt awkward when Rob was there—quiet, steady, boring Rob. No one could believe it when she upped and moved so far north to be with him.

Just as the heavy church doors were being closed, a few late mourners rushed in. I didn't bother to turn around. I wouldn't know them. The hurried, heavy footsteps stopped beside me, and a couple joined me at the end of the row. I turned and smiled. The man was like a Viking, tall, with short reddish hair and a beard. He smiled back – a warm but sad smile. The woman was petite and almost hidden behind him, but she bent forward and nodded in my direction. Her light floral perfume filled the air.

*

I dropped my car off at the hotel, so by the time I got to the wake, everyone already had a coffee or tea in their hand and a plate from the buffet. There was no queue, so nobody to start a conversation with. I grabbed a coffee and squeezed awkwardly past groups of people, amicably chatting. I wasn't sure where I was headed but kept going until I found an empty table and sank onto a sturdy wooden chair. I wondered how quickly I could make my excuses and leave. I fought the urge to get out my phone, the comfort blanket of the lonely.

I was rescued by the woman who'd joined me in the aisle at the church. She introduced herself as Hazel Henderson, a friend of Katie's, and know anyone there either. We swapped stories about how we knew Katie, and I almost choked on my tepid coffee when Hazel said they had met through a writing club.

'I didn't know she wrote. What sort of things did she write?'

'Oh, it was just for fun. She … well, we are all very shy about it. She's good, though. She won a few of our competitions, but there's never that many of us in for those!'

9

'I'm an agent. My name's Mhairi Fleming – of Fleming Jones Agency. I've known Katie since we were six. It's just strange she never said.'

'Ah, she said she had a friend who was an agent!' said Hazel sitting back and laughing. 'She was really proud of you. I urged her to send you stuff, but she really lacked confidence. She had talent, well, in my opinion. She wrote women's fiction, romance but not like Mills and Boon,' she laughed. 'Like family relationships, that sort of thing. She wrote from what she knew – from her own experience, I mean.'

I nodded and smiled. 'I wish she'd have let me see it.'

'Actually, I have a story.'

I looked up sharply. She hesitated as if contemplating whether to continue or not.

'A story she'd just finished, which you might want to look at? I could drop it off at your hotel if you like. I think you will find it interesting in the light of ...'

Before she could say any more, Rob appeared, and Hazel took that as her cue to refresh her plate. It was the first time I had had a chance to offer him my condolences, apart from briefly shaking his hand at the church. He thanked me for coming and nodded as I expressed my sadness over what had happened but remained characteristically stoic. He swiftly moved on.

Hazel came back with two plates of food, balanced on a cup of coffee. She handed me one of the plates, explaining excitedly that they'd brought out more food. I wasn't hungry but took it and thanked her.

'Oh, poor Rob,' I said. 'He looks devastated. They were so in love.'

She nodded slowly and looked as if she wanted to say something, but just then, with a bright hello, the Viking appeared. He placed a plate stacked high with sausage rolls, sandwiches, and cakes carefully on the table and then, with a smile, asked us both if we would like a drink – a real drink. I was desperate for a decent glass of white wine but felt it was rather an imposition to expect this stranger to buy it.

'It's on the house. Although I would be happy to buy you one,' he laughed and headed off to the bar before I could reply.

'Your husband?'

It was Hazel's turn to laugh.

'No, that's my little brother, Harry. Although yes – he's almost six foot and over forty, but I still call him my wee brother. Besides, he often behaves like a bairn, which is why he's so great with my kids. They adore him.'

We spoke about Hazel's children – she had three all under ten and her job – she was a schoolteacher in Beauly until Harry came back with the drinks.

'To Katie.'

We raised our glasses in a toast.

'Are you on call?' Hazel asked, pointing to his own pint of what had to be Irn Bru.

'Aye.'

'You're on call? So do you work with Rob – are you a doctor ... er surgeon?' I asked rather thrown by his appearance. He was wearing a dark tweed suit but kept pulling on his black tie and had already undone the top button of his white shirt.

'A doctor? Oh, crivens, no! Not clever enough for that. I'm a forester. And no, before you say it – I'm not a lumberjack, and I don't chop down trees. I manage forests, find markets for the timber and manage the woodcutters, as we call them, who do chop down trees and also plant lots of new ones!'

11

'Although he does wear checked shirts,' quipped Hazel.

We all laughed. They had the same warm, attractive laugh.

'I'm on call because I'm Mountain Rescue. Although, hopefully, it'll be quiet! Rob's on the team – well, he comes out now and again – it's difficult with his job. The Team Leader's err ... not able to make it, so I'm here in his place to represent the team.'

'It was Harry and the Team who found ... er, well, Katie ... well, you know,' Hazel added, then stopped, as if she'd said too much.

'Oh. That must have been traumatic – especially if you knew her. She was my friend from school – in Edinburgh. We grew up together and spent our early twenties in London. She was such fun. I can't believe she's gone.'

'She was a lovely friend.' said Hazel.

We sat in silence for a few minutes then Hazel said she had to get back for her children coming home from school. I gave her my card and told her where I was staying so she could drop off Katie's manuscript which I was keen to read. I also said, out of politeness, that I'd be interested in seeing anything she'd written. She put the card in her coat pocket and, with smiles and goodbyes, hurriedly left.

'Aye, she tells tall tales, does Hazel – no' all of them publishable!' said Harry with a wink.

'I don't know much about how Katie died,' I ventured. 'Just really what Rob told me by phone, which wasn't much. I don't even know what mountain she was on.'

He shrugged and looked uncomfortable.

'There's not much to say. It was Ben Wyvis, which is a Munro just north of here. The weather was fine – windy – but it's always windy. She was with Rob – just the two of them. She was a fair-weather

12

walker but experienced - she's climbed most of the Munros up here – which is a few. She didn't take risks. They'd made it to the summit and were walking off when she … apparently stumbled. A gust of wind caught her, and she fell .... It was in the papers.'

I realised he was upset. I felt gauche for bringing it up and reached out and touched his arm.

'Oh, that's all so sad. Poor Katie. Poor Rob. Sorry! It's just I've been away, so not seen any of the papers. Although, I doubt it would have made it into the English papers.'

He shrugged, signaling that that conversation was over.

'So, what do you do? You surely aren't a doctor?' he asked, taking a long drink.

'No! Please don't tell me your ailments … unless they are interesting! I work in London. I'm a literary agent. I try to get authors published, get them a good deal, manage their careers, that sort of thing.'

'So, we're in the same business! I help produce the paper, and you use it! Ah, so now I understand why you were talking about writing with Hazel. She's dead set on being published. I've read some of her crime stories; they're good.' He looked at me and smiled. 'Is that a bit like everyone thinking a forester cuts down trees? Everyone you meet has written a bestseller, eh?'

I laughed. I liked him. We chatted on, and then he apologised and said he'd to get back to work. He looked over at Rob, who appeared to scowl in his direction, which seemed a little odd, but he was always a strange cold creature. I decided to leave too.

I took time to say goodbye to Rob, who thanked me again for coming, as if I was there for him and not for Katie. He looked exhausted and wretched – and lost – a look I'd never seen before with Rob. He was always so confident, arrogant even. He didn't have any close family and, from what I knew, few friends. My flight wasn't until the early

13

hours of the next morning, so I half considered offering to stay and have dinner with him to make sure he ate, but I had never liked him, and he had never liked me. I always felt he resented any time Katie spent with me. I don't think he ever once asked me anything about my job or my life. He saw my work as completely trivial, which I suppose next to medicine it was, but we couldn't all save lives.

It was still early afternoon by the time I got back to the hotel. I changed out of my heels and black dress and followed the river into the town centre. My walk took me past the library, and after a moment's hesitation, I went in to read what the local papers had written about Katie's death. The initial reports were straightforward, but a few days later, the *Courier* reported that the Mountain Rescue Team Leader had raised a few questions over the nature of her death. I wondered if that was why he hadn't been at the funeral and if that accounted for Rob's disdainful look towards Harry at the wake, or was that my creative brain working overtime? I photographed the pages.

When I got back, Hazel had dropped off the manuscript. I didn't have the heart to open it on the day of her funeral. I was scared that I'd hate it.

It wasn't until I was on the 'redeye' back to London that curiosity got the better of me. My hands shook as I opened the envelope. All I could think of was Katie and how she was no longer here to laugh and tell me the story. Then the first line gave me quite a different feeling:

Most people plan parties for their fortieth birthday party. I planned to push my husband off a mountain.

It was a great start to a novel, but given the manner of Katie's death, it made my heart flutter. It told a tale of a woman driven to murder by her controlling narcissistic husband, whom everyone thought was perfect. Despite having been a senior manager at a marketing firm, as had Katie, she had lost all confidence in herself. She deferred to her husband on every decision, even on the most mundane of things, even what she wore or how she looked. She felt like the hired help – there to cook and clean to her husband's high standards.

At the end of the first chapter, I realised it was Katie's story. At the end of the novel, I wanted to kill him too. It was written as fiction, but it was too true to Katie's life. In a bizarre twist of fate, the easiest way to kill someone, she suggested, was to push him off a mountain. No witnesses.

I had gone straight to the office from the airport but left early because I couldn't concentrate on work. I re-read the newspaper reports on Katie's death on my phone and spent a restless night. My head was a jangle of twisted words and thoughts. It was quite a jump to go from accident to murder and fiction to fact. Yet Katie made little effort to hide identities or events. If I recognised it, then so would others. I couldn't help wondering if Rob knew about the manuscript. He was pompous and arrogant, but this exposed him as controlling and abusive. It would be extremely damaging to his position as Consultant Surgeon. And yet, although I didn't like him, I still couldn't see him as a murderer. The one thing I was sure of was that Rob loved her. It was fiction, I kept telling myself, it didn't prove anything, but it made me uncomfortable. How many other women were trapped in their comfortable lives like this character? It was a story that needed to be told – and what a publicity hook – the actual twist in the ending! I was getting ahead of myself. I couldn't publish this without the author. But a more serious thought came to me – should I show it to the Police? Would they believe me? It was extraordinary enough for me. And yet, if it was true if he had made Katie's life so miserable and been so worried about the exposure that he'd pushed her off a mountain – he had to face justice. I owed that to Katie and women like her.

I might have left it there, but a couple of days later, I received a chatty email from Hazel Henderson asking if I had read the manuscript and what I thought. Intriguingly she said that there was something she wanted to tell me, but it hadn't been appropriate at the funeral. She finished by mentioning that her brother Harry had asked her to ask if

I was single. That made me laugh. I replied that I was and added happily so, before deleting that and just leaving it as yes, I was single. I mentioned that I could set up a Zoom call with her over the next night or two if that suited.

I re-read Katie's story. I hadn't enough evidence to accuse Rob of murder, but I wondered if I could avenge her death by publishing the story. If I saw the similarities, so would those close to Rob. The storyline was good, but the writing needed a good bit of editing to make a decent fiction. She had all the amateur errors of too much description, all tell and no show, and lots of repetition, but the characters were well described.

It was the next night before I got a chance to Zoom with Hazel. She was in a cosy room with yellow walls and soft lighting. We chatted generally, and then we got around to Katie's manuscript. I was cautious. I explained that I liked it; it was a good story but would need some considerable editing to be published.

'So, you think you could interest a publisher?'

'I don't know, Hazel. Maybe. I have mentioned it to a guy I know at Faber, but I think it's not going to be possible without the author. What makes this interesting to me and what, quite frankly, concerns me are the parallels between Katie's life and the script? I don't know how well you knew Katie or Rob?'

Hazel took a deep breath before replying.

'Katie was unhappy. Rob was controlling, constantly finding fault in everything she did and undermining her every decision. Just like the story.'

'All the same, Hazel, it is some stretch of the imagination to go from a work of fiction to fact. Besides, it was Katie that died, not Rob.'

'Yes, but Harry often says that hillwalking is the easiest way to kill someone and get away with it. Body damaged from the fall. No witnesses.'

Katie had written that in her book.

'Besides, Dougie, the Team Leader who found Katie's body, had had concerns about her death. Harry told me. He said it was just a hunch, but based on the way she was lying and Rob's reactions at the time the body was found, Rob's story of how she fell didn't add up. He reported it to the Police. Rob was furious, raging. That's why Dougie wasn't at the funeral.'

She stopped, afraid she'd said too much, and begged me not to mention to Harry that she'd told me that. I was stunned, but not so much that I found that implausible. She was only voicing my own misgivings.

'Do you think Rob knew about the manuscript? Did she show it to him?'

Hazel took a second to answer.

'No. I don't think so. I'm pretty sure he would recognise himself, and he wouldn't like that. Katie talked about sending it to you, but,' Hazel searched for the words. 'She knew there'd be repercussions … although now she's gone … you could publish it.'

'No, like I said, without the author, it would never get past the contract stage. I'd need the approval of her executor – Rob! Besides, we are making a bit of a leap to accuse Rob of murder? We have no proof. It's a fictional story and anecdotal evidence, which isn't real evidence.'

'Oh no. I don't think we can accuse Rob of murder,' she said, suddenly alarmed. 'That's going a bit far – not with his job. What about just seeing if you can interest a publisher, and we can sort the legalities out later?'

I changed the subject, and we spoke about her family, and she asked about my job. I liked Hazel; she reminded me a little of Katie. She mentioned that Harry had asked her to pass on his phone number with a view to taking me out for dinner the next time I was in Inverness. He was too shy to ask himself. He hadn't seemed shy, but perhaps that had been bluster. I laughed and said I was very rarely in Inverness, but I would think about it. She finished by begging again that I wouldn't say anything to Harry about what she'd said about Katie's death. He'd told her in confidence, and it was a small world.

*

A week or so after the conversation with Hazel, I arranged a meeting in Inverness with a client. I didn't necessarily need to have the meeting, I could easily have done it via Zoom, but I wanted to meet Harry again. I also contacted Rob to see how he was doing and see if he'd meet for lunch or even a quick coffee when I was there. He declined lunch but agreed to meet for coffee if I went somewhere near the hospital.

Dinner with Harry was a delight until I mentioned the manuscript. The meal itself, in a little restaurant by the river, was the match of any of the best restaurants in London but half the price and more than double the table space. Harry was good-looking but not in a remarkable way; however, what he had in abundance was charm. He had a quick dry wit and constantly made me laugh. I put off mentioning Katie's death until we had left the restaurant and were having a nightcap in a cosy pub. Immediately Harry became defensive. Despite all my coaxing, all he would say was that the Team Leader had given a full report to the Police – as was standard procedure. He wouldn't say what was in it or if he, or anyone else, had any concerns. His tone made it clear that he didn't want to discuss it. I couldn't let it go. I owed that to Katie. I took a chance and told him about the manuscript and said that I thought that Rob might have murdered Katie. He flushed with anger.

'So that's why you wanted to meet me? To grill me about some fantasy story about your friend? Is this Hazel's doing? Did she put you up to this? Don't trust Hazel! Rob is on our team. Do you want me to stitch up one of our Team for murder? Do you know what you are saying? You've spent too long in your fictional world - this isn't Hamish MacBeth, this is real. Rob is a respected surgeon! Are you aware of how much damage you could do to his reputation with such wild accusations? Jesus, you are mercenary!'

At that, he finished his drink in one gulp, grabbed his coat, and, with barely a wave goodbye, stormed out of the pub. I put my head in my hands. What was I doing? I'd pushed it too far. I liked Harry. I'd blown that relationship and all for nothing. I wasn't any further finding out the truth about Katie, and he was right; it was all just speculation.

I didn't know what to do. So, I had a fictional story that I think pointed to Katie being gaslighted and then shoved off a mountain by a hero doctor. I didn't even know if Rob had read the copy which would provide the motive, and I could hardly ask him. Even if he had read it, it didn't prove anything. I knew enough about police investigations to know that I didn't have any evidence that would stand up in court. And it wasn't like Harry was likely to volunteer anything, especially not now. I had felt there was a spark there. Damn, Rob Bruce!

*

Rob was late. I was on my second latte before he arrived. He looked smart in his navy suit and had gained back the weight he had lost. He greeted me curtly and, typically, announced that he only had a short time before he'd sat down. I smiled and said I was only concerned about how he was doing. I waited until he'd nearly finished his coffee before revealing that I had a manuscript from Katie that she wanted to publish. I watched him intently for his response.

The coffee cup hovered just fractionally too long in front of his face.

'A manuscript? Or just an idea for a story?' he asked, putting the cup down slowly.

'A manuscript - a whole four hundred pages. It's good. It needs a bit of work, but I think I can get it published.'

'Well, there's no point now.'

I noticed that he hadn't asked what it was about.

'No point? Well, surely it would be a lovely tribute to Katie? A legacy to have her story in print.'

'Not without her here. So no, I don't think that's a good idea. That story doesn't belong to you. It's part of her estate. I want it returned. The paper manuscript and any files.'

'Oh, come on Rob. It's good. She wanted it published. It's why she gave it to me.'

That wasn't quite true as it had come from Hazel with no note from Katie, but he wasn't to know that.

'Yes, but she's no longer here. It's not your decision to make. It's mine.' His voice was low, but his tone was menacing, threatening.

'Don't you want to know what it's about?'

'I don't care if it's the next Nobel Prize winner. I want that manuscript sent back to me within a week, or you'll hear from my lawyer.' He pushed the cup away. 'And I thought you were her friend, Mhairi. So that was what this little chat was about. You don't really care how I am. It's just all about you and your business and making money. That's all it's been with you – your career before your friends. You want to profit from Katie's death. That's despicable.'

At that, he abruptly got up and left.

For the second time in two days, I'd been abandoned and made to feel mercenary. I felt bad, but I also knew that I was on the right track. I didn't owe Rob anything. If I didn't have staff and clients who depended on me, his attitude would have made me even more determined to publish.

I couldn't risk the business, but I didn't know what to do. I felt I owed it to Katie to go to the Police with my concerns, but would they listen? My story didn't stack up without Harry, and after the last conversation with him, I certainly wasn't going to involve him, and besides, I'd promised Hazel I wouldn't. The Police would almost certainly contact Rob, and that terrified me. He was angry enough over the manuscript. And yet Katie had reached out with that manuscript. I hadn't listened to her that last time she'd come to see me, and it was time to listen to her now.

I was back in London before I managed to track down the Police officer dealing with the case and find him on shift. I had thought I could just head into the Inverness Police Station, but these days it was all done by phone. He listened to what I had to say but didn't take a statement. I kept Harry's confidence but instead mentioned that I had read the newspaper reports and noted concerns over her death. He thanked me for my call and sought to assure me that the case had been thoroughly investigated and a report go to the Procurator Fiscal. I started to protest, but he silenced me, in a patronising manner, by explaining that it was the Fiscal's job to weigh up all the information and decide on what further action, if any, needed to be taken. The Fiscal had not raised any concerns. The case was closed.

'So, unless you have any new evidence such as a witness to the incident or a signed confession …'

I didn't let him finish. I tersely thanked him and closed the call. I had a pile of work to do, but my heart wasn't in it.

The next morning, a note came in from a publisher to say they were interested in Katie's manuscript, if I could use the tragic story of her death to promote it. But before I could weigh that up, an email came from Rob's lawyer requesting the return of the manuscript. The email left me in no doubt that my reputation and that of my company would suffer if I didn't comply. I sent it back - keeping a copy, of course. I hadn't heard from Harry. It was all for nothing.

I felt I had let Katie and women like her down.

It was almost November when I heard from Hazel. She asked if I had managed to get a publisher interested in the story. I replied that yes, I had a publisher who'd shown some interest but that Rob had demanded the return of the manuscript, so my hands were tied.

'I have something to confess,' she said. 'I wrote the story. It was never Katie's.'

A note from the author:

'Friends and Foes,' originally titled 'Invisible Ink,' came from a class exercise on writing codes to signify genre. I chose the church scene option, which coincided with the funeral of the father of one of my oldest school friends. At the funeral, I was struck by the fact that I had known my friend, her parents, and siblings since I was five but knew hardly anyone else at the service, which gave me my opening. I also planned my story idea out, which I admit being entirely skeptical about, but it did help form the plot. The ending came from a fellow student's feedback, suggesting that a short story works better with a twist. She was right! Although I do plan to write the full version, incorporating chapters of Katie's manuscript, to highlight the silent trauma of a stifling relationship. One to look out for in the future.

Catherine Halliday studied BA (Hons) Creative Writing at the University of the Highlands and Islands 2019-2023. Originally from Edinburgh, she now lives in Lossiemouth, Moray. www.catherinehalliday.co.uk Twitter:@WriterCHalliday

Terra Firma

Geoff King

In her recurring dream, Captain Lisa Umfadi always finds herself advancing through the tunnels of the dormant volcano, confident no threat remains. The deeper she goes, the more she sweats and struggles for breath, a sign this mountain still simmers in its sleep. This time, following the lights strung along the main passageway, she finally reaches a vast cavern – the centre of the rebel base.

She stops. The alarm system still flashes and wails, but everyone is dead.

Hundreds of bodies carpet the ground, all with their eyes wide in shock, blood leaking from their noses and ears. All unarmed. All women and children.

Knotted thorns twist in her gut. Unable to wrench her eyes from the carnage, she drops her blaster and sinks to her knees. I did this, she thinks.

Lisa woke with a start, panting and tangled in sweaty sheets. A cold hand prodded her shoulder. Shrill ringing drilled into her ears.

'There is someone at the door, Lisa,' said Zari, nudging her again.

She took a deep breath. 'No shit.'

'Shall I answer it for you?'

Lisa groaned and peered at the clock. She blinked a few times to clear the blur. *Six a.m. for fuck's sake.*

'No.' The ringing stopped. 'If it's important, they'll come back later.'

Zari waited next to the bed. 'Are you getting up now, Lisa?'

'Not a chance.' Lisa squinted up into Zari's glowing amber eyes. 'Deactivate.'

The droid's head drooped, and her lights dulled to silver grey.

The doorbell sounded again. Her first day back on Earth after a two-year mission, and already someone had come to bother her. Space-lag sucked. So did this hangover. She'd have to endure another week of disorientation before she felt normal again, aside from her injuries; they would take longer to heal. The battle that followed the failed negotiations was long and brutal. Lisa was lucky to survive with a broken arm, fractured ribs, and laser burns. She pulled the covers over her head and sank into oblivion.

*

Once more, Zari poked Lisa's shoulder and wrenched her from sleep.

'It's time to get up now, Lisa.'

'Will you stop that?' She slapped the droid's hand away. 'I thought I turned you off.' She sipped some water from the bedside table; it had gone tepid overnight. The open-plan apartment, despite its size, smelled airless and clammy.

'Due to safety override protocols, personal droids for officers reactivate every two hours.'

'Oh, great. What's the time?'

'Oh-eight hundred hours.'

'You're a massive pain in the arse, you know that?' Lisa flopped back on the pillow. 'No offence, but I didn't ask for a PD.'

'I'm sorry if I cause you pain, Lisa. Star Force assigned me to you for—'

'I know, I know. But can't you just let me sleep?' It felt like a fist was battering the inside of her skull. 'Anyway, I'm on leave. Go away.'

'I'm sorry, Lisa, I must disobey your request on this occasion. You have a debriefing session with Colonel Kronos in one hour and fifteen minutes.'

'Not going.'

'Your attendance is obligatory.'

'And you're going to make me go?'

'No, Lisa. My programming will not allow me to physically coerce a human. However, Star Force is authorised to withhold one month's salary for non-attendance.'

Bastards. Lisa hit the pillow and growled.

Star Force provided Zari on Lisa's return to Earth, ostensibly as a reward for Outstanding Service on Epsilon 5. She suspected it was more to keep an eye on her. Despite the successful outcome of the operation, Major Veltos reported her to be "a loose cannon who cannot always be relied upon to follow orders," and in his opinion, "her reckless behavior, due to unresolved emotional trauma, imperiled the mission and endangered the lives of the entire unit."

Arse. What did he know anyway? He'd neither been there nor seen active duty for twenty years. What happened was tragic, but she kept telling herself it wasn't her fault.

'Why is it so hot in here?' Lisa threw back the bedding. 'Activate the air-con, will you?'

'I'm sorry, Lisa, the air conditioning unit has malfunctioned. I have notified the maintenance team, and they promised to send an operative within seven working days.'

'Great. I sacrifice everything for Star Force and The Overseers, and they can't even keep my apartment maintained.' Lisa raised herself on one elbow and gestured across the room. 'Just open a window, will you?'

The screens slid up, and sunlight sliced into Lisa's eyes. She shielded her face with her free arm. The hard cast whacked her in the forehead.

'Ow! Damn stupid bloody arm.'

'Can I be of assistance, Lisa?'

'No.' She tried to sit up. Earth gravity dragged at her like a suit of leadcrete.

'May I suggest some liquid rehydration salts to alleviate the effects of alcohol poisoning?'

Pain pounded through Lisa's head, obliterating her thoughts. It felt like someone was squeezing and releasing her eyes repeatedly. Even the roots of her teeth throbbed. On top of that, her whole body ached, and her mouth tasted like a rat's piss.

'No. Just make me a good strong coffee.'

Zari glided to the kitchen area on silent castors and opened a cupboard.

'I'm sorry, Lisa,' she said. 'There is no coffee. Would you like tea?'

'You must be joking. What good would that do me?'

'Tea is a hydrating beverage, can improve muscle endurance, has high oxygen radical absorbance capacity—'

'Enough! I don't want tea. Nor do I want a talking encyclopedia.' Lisa rubbed her face and took a few deep breaths. 'Go get more coffee from the shop across the street.'

'I'm sorry, Lisa. The elevator is temporarily out of service, and I am unable to navigate the stairs.'

'Wonderful.' Lisa eased her legs over the side of the bed and waited a few moments for a wave of nausea to pass.

'I have notified the maintenance team, and—'

'Let me guess: 'they've promised to send an operative within seven working days'.'

'Yes, Lisa. That is correct.'

There were times when Lisa regretted her decision to live in Historyville. Somehow, its quaint charms just felt more *Earthy* when she returned from space, but the retro appeal wore thin when the equipment failed. It was all reproduction anyway; maybe old technology needed to actually *be* old to work properly.

On the table by the sofa, a half-empty bottle of whisky lay next to a dog-eared photograph. Lisa stood, swayed slightly, and stumbled through her discarded clothes to the table. She picked up the picture and slumped onto the sofa. Her and Lianne, both grinning, the day they got engaged. Lisa's eyes began to sting. She bit her lip and blinked. A single tear splashed onto Lianne's face. A few seconds later, the bottle was halfway to her lips.

'It is not recommended to consume alcohol at this time of the morning,' said Zari from behind her. 'I must also advise you that Colonel Kronos will disapprove if you arrive at his office in an inebriated state.'

'Is that a fact?' Lisa leaned back into the cushions and looked at the bottle. 'Fuck.' She screwed the lid back on and slammed it on the table.

'Get me some PainAway,' she said. 'Then find me a clean uniform while I get showered.'

Zari returned with a bottle of pills and a fresh glass of water and stood over Lisa like an overbearing mother ensuring her child took the full dose of medicine.

Ten minutes later, Lisa was washed and dressed. Although her vision remained fuzzy, the analgesic had kicked in and reduced the pain to tolerable levels.

Next, buy coffee.

She opened the apartment door, stepped through, and tripped over a box. Automatically thrusting out her injured arm, it gave way beneath her, and her head slammed onto the floorboards. She yelled in pain and rolled onto her back. The world spun. With her eyes screwed shut, she lay still and waited for the world to settle down.

'Do you require medical assistance, Lisa?' asked Zari's toneless voice.

With her left hand on the wall for balance, Lisa inched herself upright. 'No. Just take the box inside, will you?'

'Shall I open it for you, Lisa?' Zari picked up the box.

'Is it addressed to you?'

'No. It is addressed to Captain Lisa Umfadi.'

'Well then.' If Lisa was going to keep this droid, it would need some serious reprogramming to avoid it sending her insane. 'Go back inside and put the box on the table.'

Thankfully, there was only one flight of stairs; Lisa grabbed the handrail and made her way down to the front door. The latest droids had no problem negotiating steps; no doubt she'd been given an obsolete model because it was cheap. Star Force was continually streamlining since The Overseers awarded them the contract for off-planet security, anything to satisfy the shareholders' rapacious greed and the directors' hunger for bigger bonuses.

Out on the street, Lisa squinted and shaded her eyes. The dome kept the fumes out, but the unfiltered sunlight glared off every surface. It was good to be back on Earth, in the suburb where she was born. The artfully recreated stone and redbrick buildings looked just like they did in the ancient film files; the transpods spoiled the effect, though. She waited for a gap in the traffic; even in Historyville, commuters zoomed by on their way to whatever mind-numbing employment they had mortgaged their souls for. As the last pod hovered past, she trudged across the road and into the shop. Her favorite brand of coffee sat on its usual shelf, but old Gregg was no longer there to berate her for not taking proper care of herself. He died a month ago, and the place had been automated. Baffled by the new checkout, Lisa waved her wrist chip at the scanner. Nothing happened.

Stupid bloody thing! She was tempted to leave without paying, but the hassle of getting her account reactivated wasn't worth it. She tried again; this time, the machine beeped and displayed the message, 'Insufficient funds – please contact your financial service provider.'

What the fuck? You have to be shitting me! My credits should have registered as soon as I landed. Lisa took out her com to call the bank.

The shop disappeared in a blue-white flash, and a colossal thump slammed her into the counter. Her legs gave way, and she slid to the floor.

After a moment of blackness, Lisa lifted her head, stunned and disoriented. It felt like her back was on fire. Whimpering, she grabbed the countertop and dragged herself to her feet, lungs straining to find oxygen. Globules of molten glass pocked the surface, each spawning a tiny wisp of smoke. Half-melted packets slumped on the shelves like deflated balloons. Fumes tinged with scorched flesh, singed hair, and burnt plastic thickened the air. She rubbed her forehead; her fingers came away wet with blood. Beyond the rumble filling her ears, muffled screams echoed from the street.

Lisa turned. The shop windows were missing. She swayed for a moment and staggered outside, hardly able to bear the pain. Blackened bodies writhed and jerked amongst the overturned pods. In the middle of the road, Zari's head rocked as it settled amongst shattered glass. Lisa looked up. There was a massive hole where her apartment should have been. Flames roared from the gaping maw like dragon fire through jagged teeth, and dark fumes belched into the sky. Dizziness overwhelmed her, and she collapsed onto the street.

*

The cushioned face-rest pressed into Lisa's cheekbones; she stared at the spotless slate-grey tiles – her view until the NooSkin healed the burns on her back. It felt like a blanket of stinging jellyfish. The cloying tang of SteriMax prickled her nostrils and clawed at the back of her throat. After only twelve hours lying on her front, her breasts felt uncomfortably squashed – no doubt this purpose-built bed was designed by a man. Or if she'd shelled out for Premium Healthcare, the hospital may have provided a softer mattress.

Her photo was gone, destroyed in the blast; likewise, all her stored images and files. Would she eventually forget Lianne's face? She'd carried that photo with her for two years, wallowing in her grief, allowing her anger to build and fester like an abscess until it burst and poisoned her decision-making. She'd learnt her lesson at a terrible cost and now bore the burden of guilt and regret arising from her actions – with plenty of time to think about it. Although still plagued by nightmares on the long journey home, Star Force refused to pay for her counseling.

And now this. No one had come to tell her what had happened. She didn't want to know. Though her mind remained fuzzy, she remembered the box...and the screams of the people dying in the street.

Above the buzzing, beeping meditech, and lobotomizing Muzak, Lisa heard the approaching thud of military boots. A pair of polished, black toecaps appeared by her bed.

Go away, she thought.

Someone cleared their throat.

'Captain Umfadi.' Colonel Kronos's unmistakable voice pounded off the walls like a thunderclap. 'You had a lucky escape.'

'But you're here anyway, sir,' said Lisa, thinking of the meeting she'd missed.

Kronos was quiet for a moment. 'I meant, if you had stayed in your apartment you would have been vaporised.'

'Well, I've got the droid to thank for that. If she could've negotiated the stairs, I wouldn't have gone out for coffee.'

'Well, you'll be pleased to hear we can refabricate it.'

'Zari? Wasn't she destroyed in the blast?'

'Only the body. The hard drive is bombproof – all that data is too valuable to lose.'

'Thanks, but don't bother on my account; I've managed thirty-one years without one.'

Kronos ignored her comment. 'This time, you'll get the latest model, with fully-operable legs.'

Lisa didn't feel comfortable talking to Kronos without being able to read his face. His rugged, emotionless voice gave little away, but his eyes couldn't hide his feelings. Knowing she shouldn't, Lisa eased herself onto all fours. Sitting back on her heels, she gasped as the skin on her back tightened. Kronos looked down at her with a furrowed brow. Straight and tall as she remembered, he'd aged considerably since she last saw him, despite his unfeasibly black hair. The lines in his face looked hacked out with a chisel, and his flinty eyes had receded deeper into shadowed sockets, like stones sinking into the mud. Spotless and pristine, his uniform looked fresh from the fabricator; it probably was. His gaze wandered up and down her body in the thin hospital gown.

With a small sigh and a shake of her head, Lisa crossed her arms. 'Do you know who did it?'

'No one's yet claimed responsibility,' said Kronos, looking away, 'but it's got Tzakan Freedom Alliance written all over it.'

Lisa closed her eyes and tried to hold back the surge of boiling hate that seethed through her at the mention of the TFA. After a short silence, she took a deep breath, but her voice grated when she spoke.

'Why target me? I'm only a captain.'

Kronos's brow furrowed. 'If you'd stayed on the base as we advised,' he said, 'they wouldn't have got to you, but with the lack of security in Historyville, you were an easy target.'

'But I've never even been to Tzakan.'

'You're regarded as a military hero, a conqueror of rebels. To the TFA, you represent The Overseers' political authority and the military force you've sworn allegiance to. And, as I said, an easy target.' He glanced around and sank into the chair in the corner of the room. This was a bad sign. Kronos wasn't just here to see how she was.

Lisa didn't feel up to a long conversation; NooSkin worked wonders but required a great deal of the body's reserves. 'Well, The Overseers and Star Force have lost my allegiance now. After what happened on Epsilon 5, I've sworn never to bear weapons again.'

Kronos brushed a speck of dust from his trousers. 'Acting on the intel provided, you did what you had to.'

32

'The intel was the difficulty.' The media relished reporting the victory over the insurgents, but Star Force's press department withheld the problematic half of the story.

'Nevertheless, you still have nine months remaining on your contract before you're free to be released from duty.'

Bastards. Even after twelve years of service and all she'd just been through, they were still going to milk her for every ounce of contractual obligation. 'I told you – I won't fight anymore. And you can't make me serve.'

'You won't have to, and yes, we can. Unless you want to spend the rest of your commission in the lunar penitentiary.' Kronos shifted his weight in the chair as if uncomfortable with this threat. The buttons on his jacket flashed like miniature suns. 'We're sending you on a non-combat mission. Part of a delegation to negotiate with the Tzakani.'

Lisa almost leaped off the bed. 'You must be fucking kidding me,' she said through gritted teeth. Of all the colonies in the galaxy, why would they send her there? 'They've just bombed my apartment, and you know they killed—'

Kronos held up a hand. 'Yes. I know.' He stood, and his eyes flashed as he looked down at her. 'But I would remind you that you're talking to your commanding officer, and it would be advisable to adjust your tone.'

Lisa bit her lip and lowered her eyes. 'Yes...sir.'

'The Tzakani government has distanced itself from the terrorists. The negotiations will include a requirement for them to disarm the rebels themselves. And after your recent ... erm, *noteworthy* performance, your presence will remind them of what can happen if diplomacy fails.'

'I'm not going to repeat what happened on Epsilon 5, but I also don't know if I'll be able to keep my temper. It's a barely disguised secret that half of Tzakan's politicians used to be in the TFA.'

'There's no proof of that, but if you identify some individuals while you're there, we could press for their incarceration. That would make our job easier.' Kronos took his pad from his pocket and swiped up the holoscreen. 'The mission is outlined here. You'll get more detail once you're out of the hospital.'

Lisa scanned the brief and looked into Kronos's eyes. 'I've never negotiated without a gun in my hands.'

'Don't worry.' He stared back. 'The rest of the delegation will oversee the talks.'

'I really don't like this.' Lisa sighed and shook her head.

'You don't have like it, but you have to go nonetheless.'

Why won't he piss off and leave me alone? she thought.

Kronos moved over to the window. Below the battleship-grey sky, an ocean of smog spread beneath the hospital tower, mottled with glows from the lights below. A few dozen skyscrapers waded into the distance, pinnacles of prestige where the elite and powerful could breathe cleaner air. Beyond them, Histoyville's dome protruded like a giant bubble in a sea of foam.

'There's another reason you're sending me, isn't there?' said Lisa.

'Very perceptive.' He turned back to look at her. 'We need one of our own to keep an eye on the other envoys. Intel suggests there may be a mole in the delegation. We need you to play your part and observe them carefully and um ... surreptitiously.' He said the last word as if he believed Lisa incapable of that.

'Spy, you mean?'

'Exactly. Befriend them, put them at their ease, and by the time you get to Tzakan, you'll have gained their trust.'

Lisa smiled humourlessly. 'I'm not known for my social skills, and I have no experience in espionage.'

'You can practice the former, and you'll be trained for the latter. Your droid will record conversations and interpret body language, and facial expressions—'

'And she'll be spying on me as I spy on them.'

'More of an assistant...or advisor.'

'Yeah, same thing.'

'Not exactly...'

Lisa started to feel lightheaded and swayed a little. 'I'm sorry, sir, I have to lie down again.' She lowered herself onto the bed and put her face back in the rest. 'What are we supposed to be negotiating anyway.'

'The evacuation of Tzakan,' he said in a matter-of-fact voice.

'Of who? And why?'

'The entire population...' Kronos paused. 'We're going to destroy their planet.'

*

The delegation should have met the day before the SF Avantar launched, but events moved forward much faster than anticipated. According to The Overseers' astronomers, the comet would pass Tzakan in a matter of weeks. The deflection caused by Tzakan's gravity would put it on a collision course with Hubworld, the galaxy's largest settlement. If Tzakan were destroyed, the comet would pass through the system without causing harm. Unfortunately, a vast majority of Tzakan's inhabitants continued to resist the evacuation.

'I would let them die on their own turf if that's what they want,' Kronos had said, 'and save the effort and expense of sending a ship to dissuade a bunch of intransigent colonists from committing suicide.'

Lisa agreed. She'd never forgive the TFA for what they'd done, and she couldn't believe the government of Tzakan, with its openly separatist stance, had no connection with the terrorists. Yet here she was on this ridiculous mission to try to save their lives. At least she wouldn't have to kill anyone this time, though the prospect of a diplomatic assignment promised to be more boring than AI poetry.

Once the ship reached cruising speed, Lisa navigated her way to the conference room. The door hissed open, and she stepped inside. Lacking confidence in negotiating skills, she had to present a convincing front from the outset; in Lisa's experience, showing weakness or doubt in a group always lost their respect.

Three people sat around an oval table, with space for several more; at least she wasn't late.

She nodded, 'Captain Lisa Umfadi reporting for duty. I've been—'

A tall woman with oriental features stood so quickly her chair fell over behind her. She scowled at Lisa with her large teeth bared before turning to address a bald man on her right. 'There's no place for a cold-blooded murderer in negotiations as delicate as this,' she barked.

Lisa looked from one to the other, lost for words. Surely, this stranger couldn't possibly know the truth about her last mission? But that was the only explanation she could think of. She would have to be careful how she responded to this. *It wasn't my fault* it would sound defensive, pathetic even. It was going to be a challenging mission with this kind of hostility within the team.

The man raised his hands. 'Please sit down and calm yourself, Doctor Lee. You are exaggerating, and Captain Umfadi has been appointed as Space Force's official representative, approved by The Overseers themselves. We will need to work together if we are to succeed in our undertaking.' The dark dome of his head reflected the cool white lights as he turned to face Lisa. She couldn't help wondering if he polished it in front of the mirror every morning.

'Welcome, Captain Umfadi,' he continued. 'I'm Jonah Celcus, Earth Parliament's special envoy, appointed as chair for all our discussions. Doctor Angong Lee is our science officer, specialising in astrobiology, morphogenesis, and quantum evolution.'

Lee retrieved her chair, sat, and crossed her arms, scowling at Lisa like she was something unflushable in the toilet bowl. Lisa decided to ignore her.

'Numa Loscher,' Celcus indicated a plump, androgynous Caucasian who fidgeted in a revolving chair, 'is our chief negotiator. Numa has many years experience – and much success – in arbitration with former colonies.'

'Pleased to meet you, Captain,' said Loscher with a lop-sided smile. 'Your reputation precedes you.'

'So it seems,' said Lisa, unsure if Loscher referred to Lee's outburst or the officially released version of events.

'Please take a seat, Lisa.' Celcus pulled out the chair next to him. 'Can I call you Lisa? I think we'll all get along better if we use first names, don't you?'

'Whatever you say, Jonah.' Lisa ignored the chair and took one at the far end of the table. 'Sorry, I don't like sitting with my back to the door – old habit.'

'Don't you have a PD with you?' asked Celcus. 'You are welcome to bring it to our meetings.'

'Yes. But that won't be necessary.' Kronos had insisted Zari accompany Lisa everywhere she went, but he wasn't here. 'I've left her in my cabin.'

'Her?' Numa Loscher's eyebrows arched as if they'd been pulled up by strings.

'It's my first droid,' said Lisa, trying not to sound apologetic. 'Well, rebuilt actually. I thought if I assigned a gender, I'd relate to it more easily, especially if she's going to share my cabin.'

Loscher sniggered. 'ow quaint.'

'The others should arrive shortly,' said Celcus. 'In addition to our negotiating team, we have four bodyguards to watch our backs on Tzakan.'

'Only four?' Angong Lee frowned. 'That won't be much good to us if the TFA attack. Unless Captain Carnage here has brought her sonic mortars...'

'Now, now, Doctor. You know Lisa has renounced violence. As for the guards, we already have two thousand regulars on the planet to coordinate the evacuation. And you'll be pleased to know – though it makes me slightly nervous – in addition to the arks, there are four battle-ready destroyers in orbit.' Celcus rubbed his hand over his head as if to smooth down his nonexistent hair and looked at Lisa. 'The SF Avantar has twelve crew, but you will have little to do with them. We share the rec room and canteen, so you can introduce yourself if you wish.'

Over the next few minutes, the remaining four members of the team joined them; Celcus introduced them each in turn. Lisa got the feeling they all knew each other before the mission, which put her at a disadvantage. The sooner she worked out the relationships and dynamics between them, the easier her job would be.

'And this,' continued Celcus as the final delegate arrived, 'is Aphren Adams, psychologist, and anthropologist.'

As their eyes met, both Lisa and Adams smiled. Lisa felt a warm flush ripple through her chest – something she'd not felt since Lianne died. Adams was strikingly attractive, with a face reminiscent of an Icelandic princess from an epic saga: high cheekbones, aquamarine eyes, and short, spiky hair as dark as deep space. They nodded to each other wordlessly. Lisa swallowed and turned back to Celcus.

He took his pad from his pocket and swiped up a display in the centre of the table. 'Now to business. We have a lot to discuss.'

*

After the meeting, which proved as tedious as she'd expected, Lisa returned to her cabin. Zari's head lifted, and her eyes glowed.

'Can I be of assistance, Lisa?'

The voice was the same, the personality unchanged, but now Zari looked a little more human. Lisa found the upgraded version easier to talk to; the BioFlex skin was more convincing than the stiff hemplas of the previous model, and this one could walk, even if its movements were a little jerky. She found it incredible that scientific progress was still so far behind the fiction. The vintage sci-fi she watched as a youth depicted far more advanced tech than available now, and some of those films were over two centuries old. Still, at least Zari now had improved software and four-star security clearance to the next.

'Yes,' said Lisa. 'You can tell me how Angong Lee knows about what happened on Epsilon 5. I thought that was classified; Space Force fed the media a story of my 'heroic battle against barbaric rebels'.'

'Of course, Lisa. I will examine all relevant data streams and report momentarily.'

Lisa flopped on her narrow bunk and stared at the ceiling, thankful her back no longer hurt.

A moment later, Zari spoke again. 'I have detected a leak to the media twelve hours and thirty-six minutes ago. I traced the source to the office of the Space Force security department, but I have been unable to identify the individual responsible because several agents share the same interface.'

'Shit.' Lisa sat up. 'This is serious. Kronos needs to know. Can you send him a message?'

'He knows already.'

'What? Why didn't he tell me?'

'I'm sorry, Lisa, I cannot access that information. The personal motivation of absent individuals can only be hypothesised by speculation. Unless I can hear the tone of voice or interpret facial expressions, my understanding is insufficient to deduce the reasons influencing human behavior and m—'

'Stop. It was a rhetorical question.'

'In that case, Lisa, may I suggest that in the future you indicate which questions are rhetorical so you do not have to endure unnecessary responses.'

Oh, give me a break. 'You can suggest it, but I may not remember.'

'In that case, Lisa, I can recommend some psychological exercises that will enhance your memory skills.'

For fuck's sake! 'No thanks. Deactivate.'

A single cabin on a space flight was a luxury afforded only to officers and dignitaries. Lisa was thankful not to be sharing; she needed quiet time alone to think. The attraction she'd felt to Aphren Adams provoked a stab of guilt. She reached for the photo in her top pocket.

Of course, it wasn't there. Now, she would never see Lianne's face again, but she would always remember their final words, a little over two years ago...

The revolving restaurant turned slowly, its wide windows exhibiting the star-filled expanse above. With lights pulsing beneath the sea of fumes, it looked like they hovered above radioactive soup. A soft babble of voices drifted through the room, floating on waves of aroma: sizzling steaks, braised vegetables, seared fish.

Lianne placed a hand on top of Lisa's. 'Please don't go.' Her eyes sparkled with moisture. 'Why do you have to charge into every dangerous situation? It's like you have a death wish.'

'I enjoy the thrill, and I'm doing some good – it's for the betterment of the human race.' Lisa shrugged and swigged her wine. 'You used to like that about me. You said I was your "space hero". What's changed?'

'I know it's what first attracted me to you, but I love you now.' Lianne's voice trembled a little. 'And I don't want you to get hurt.'

The waiter whirred up to their table and cleared the plates. 'Would you like to order desserts?'

Lisa waved him away, took both Lianne's hands in hers and squeezed. 'I love you too,' she said, still endeared by the galaxy of freckles across Lianne's cheeks and her alluring emerald eyes. 'And I'm going to miss you like hell. But it's my job, Lianne. I'm a soldier. It's what I do. You knew that before we...before things between us got serious. And I've always made clear my ambition to make colonel one day, and this is a step towards that.'

'But you've never been gone for so long before.' Lianne bit her lip. 'You told me you're allowed to turn down one mission in your career. You never have. So this time, I'm asking you not to go.' Tears trickled down her cheeks. 'Please.'

Why was she making this so difficult? 'I'm perfect for this operation. That's why they chose me. Don't you realise what an honour it is to command a battalion? This could give me the promotion I've worked towards for so long.' Lisa released Lianne's hands and poured herself a fourth glass of wine. 'Anyway, we've been through this before. It's who I am.' She downed half the glass in one gulp. 'Don't ask me to change who I am.'

'But—'

'And I don't like feeling trapped.'

'Is that what I am to you – a trap?'

Lisa sighed. 'I didn't mean it like that.' Lianne could be so sensitive; it was like walking on eggshells. 'You know they say emotional dependency is unhealthy? It could be a chance for you to process your abandonment issues.'

'Oh, so now you're saying a lengthy separation will be good for our relationship?' Lianne gazed through the window, up at the stars. 'I think you'd rather be out there than here with me.' She shook her head. 'All those action movies you watched as a kid – they were supposed to provide entertainment, not role models.' She looked back into Lisa's eyes. *Was it sadness or pity?* 'You've become a walking cliché.'

Lisa glared across at her. 'Thanks, Lianne. That's just what I needed to hear on our last night together for two years.' She slammed her hands on the table and knocked over the last of her wine, which soaked into the white tablecloth like a pool of blood. The glass rolled off the table and shattered on the floor.

Lisa stood and stormed out of the restaurant. That night, she stayed on the base.

There was no time to make amends or say goodbye before the ship launched the next morning. As they moved beyond Earth's gravity, a personal message came through for Lisa in her cabin:

At oh-nine-twenty hours this morning, the TFA initiated a terrorist attack on the offices of the Offworld Ministry. I regret to inform you that, having just reached her workstation, Lianne Arossa was amongst the many fatalities. I am sorry for your loss. In sympathy, Colonel Kronos.

Captain Lisa Umfadi went into stasis like an injured lamb and came out like a wounded tiger.

Forest at Night

Geoff King

The sun surrenders, swallowed into the belly of the Earth, and homeward bound I enter the woods. Indigo spilt on the eastern skyline seeps imperceptibly into space.

The first stars stipple the twilight, diamonds on darkening velvet. I shiver as the owl's hoot heralds the hunting hour; their prey busy below the creaking canopy, scuttling through humus and underbrush, rustling dry leaves and grass stems, snatching furtive snacks.

Trees with crooked crowns gather, lean together and huddle, smudge their shadows into dark foggy curtains, confer in covert whispers, and hide mysteries beneath their skirts. The forest wafts moths from its woven walls, exhaling a tang of night-time: sharp, crisp, cold; musky and sweet; soil, leaf mould and moss, honeysuckle, fungi and fern, pine needles and birch breath.

Genetic memories remain, stirring fear of creatures no longer here. Once the domain of wolf, lynx and bear, now deer run rampant; stags' bellows shake boughs, loud enough to stun hinds into surrender for the procreation of a new generation. Thriving lives, spectacles of Nature's elegant embroidery, perform for an arboreal audience, indifferent to the drama and gathered into the blanket of night, concealed from diurnal sight.

I reach the shelter of my home and hearth, and night is swallowed into the belly of the Earth.

A note from the author:

I wrote the first 1300 words of *Terra Firma* as a creative writing exercise, 'Writing Beginnings and Endings', in my second year from the prompt, 'Write about a character being awoken from a dream or a nightmare.' In fourth year, we were asked to share the start of a novel for feedback. I was reading science fiction at the time and remembered this piece. I made a rough plan of the novel's plot and expanded the piece to 5500 words, envisaging a sci-fi mystery with intrigue, injustice, government corruption and corporate exploitation, while exploring themes of grief, guilt, greed and trauma through a single point-of-view character. I've tried to raise questions in the reader's mind to keep them reading: What really happened on Epsilon 5? Who are The Overseers? How will Lisa contain her suppressed anger in negotiations with the Tzakani? Can Zari be trusted?

'Forest at Night' was originally written in response to an exercise as part of a Wild Ways to Writing course led by Helen Moore. The brief was to take a walk at night away from artificial light and explore the darkness with all the senses. The original poem was laid out in stanzas, but after feedback I transformed it into a prose poem.

Geoff King studied Creative Writing BA (Hons) at the University of the Highlands and Islands 2019 – 23. He has self-published two novels and has work in The Rabbit Hole: Weird Stories Volume One, scififantasynetwork.com, Earth Pathways Diary *and* Atlas Poetica. *In addition to* Terra Firma, *he is currently working on a novel for older teenagers. Twitter:* @WoodTreasures; *Facebook:* www.facebook.com/Geoff.F.King; *Website and blog:* www.geoffkingwriter.co.uk

Noriko

S. J. Milne

Dismounting the bus upon arriving in Kyoto, I found myself alone and shaking. No other passengers had dared brave the long, hot journey from morning until late afternoon - scared off by the many near misses caused by the approach speed on treacherously narrow corners. While the driver had politely collected my luggage from the vehicle's belly, I wondered if his greying hair was caused by age or the constant risk of death on the road. Bidding him farewell, I made a note on my phone to check whether he would be my escort home; if so, I would need to search for other alternatives.

The Kyoto air was different from that of Tokyo's. Almost sweet, like candied bamboo and chestnuts. Having come to escape the frustrations of painting and family pressures to get married for the sole purpose of producing a son, it seemed like a good omen that the stale taste of industry was behind me. Mount Minako sat proudly in the near-distance, casting a long shadow towards my destination. The bus station was scarcely more than a wooden hut manned by a young boy who had fallen asleep in his booth, the pages of his open workbook fluttering in the warm breeze. He reminded me of myself at that age, although I can't recall ever doing homework. I pulled out my phone to check for directions, but it sadly stared back at me with a whirling circle, no bars, and an almost non-existent percentage. Sighing, I stuffed the device back in my pocket. I tightened the straps of my backpack before picking up my over-sized duffle, walking in the direction of a signpost. My brow crinkled in the sunlight while I squinted at the individual arrows, 3 miles, 6 miles, 10 miles, and at the bottom there was an old, polished wooden sign with beautiful white paint stating 'Ikigai House, first left, 0.4 miles'.

Relief patted my back as I walked off in the right direction, heading up a rough path through thick trees that carried the heady scent of summer. It wasn't long before the Ryokan came into view. The main building emanated an old rustic charm but was well-maintained with a welcoming allure. My breath was uneven when I reached the door, suggesting my non-active lifestyle might need to change. Without the chance to collect myself, the door swung open, revealing an entranceway with a bright interior and an awaiting staff of four, all dressed in matching muted attire.

'Welcome,' they said in unison, ushering me into the building, taking my bags and jacket while I attempted to stifle my ragged breathing.

Looking down, a stunning young woman, wrapped in a brightly patterned kimono with her dark hair snuggled up neatly behind her head, exposing her neck, lay down a soft pair of slippers and smiled at me expectantly. *Woah.* I caught myself staring and forced my eyes away; I used my heels to force my shoes off and slid my feet into their new home. The softly-dressed staff bustled around before disappearing, leaving me with the young woman.

'Mr Usui?'

A voice from the far end of the foyer drew my attention; I could see an elderly lady standing behind a desk. Making my way over, the kimono woman followed closely enough for me to notice the fragrance of the oils used on her skin.

'Welcome to Ikigai House, Mr Usui. We expect to host you for three nights, is that correct?'

'Yes,' I replied.

'Excellent, this is your welcome package and your room number,' she said, laying out a folder and a wooden block with a string tied to the top. I looked at the block in surprise. Noticing my expression, the clerk added, 'As the Ryokan has been kept as authentically traditional as possible, the rooms are separated by shoji-style doors. However, you do not need to be concerned about security as the safety of our patrons is our priority. Additionally, no other guests are rooming at our establishment at the moment, so you can be at ease and use any facilities at your leisure.'

'Thank you,' I said, picking up the "key". 'Can I go to my room now?'

'Of course.' The elderly woman smiled, her face seeming youthful, and beckoned to the young woman by my side. 'This is Noriko. She is a Nakai at our establishment and has been selected to serve you throughout your stay. She will lead you to your room, and if you have any questions, please don't hesitate to ask her.'

I followed Noriko, charmed by the short intervals between her steps. As we walked, my gaze continuously drifted toward where her posterior would be located - if it could be seen through the thick layers of clothing wrapped around her. *Stop looking, you idiot; she'll notice.* She led me through the main property and out to a building that stood on the other side of a large pond. Once inside, Noriko navigated a long, twisting wooden corridor before stopping at a paper door. She knelt and slid the door open in one deft movement, politely motioning for me to enter. The room was large and pleasant, containing everything I expected of a traditional Japanese-style room: low wooden tables with cushions for sitting, an evident indoor non-tatami area beside a wall-sized window called an engawa, and a large display unit built into the far corner. Glancing around, I searched for my sleeping accommodation, hoping a short doze would wash away the horrors of the earlier bus ride from hell. Noriko glided to a large in-built cupboard and opened the doors.

'The futon is stored within this double cupboard during the day; I shall prepare it for you at night. Would you like it now, Mr Usui?'

Noriko's Kyoto accent was thick and melodious. Her words sounded as if she spoke in slow cursive; it was attractive yet formal, an odd combination.

'Yes, I would like to rest.'

Leaving Noriko to set up the futon, I wandered the large room, glancing through the glass window-wall of the engawa hidden by a half-expanded bamboo screen. The indoor veranda's floor was boarded and cool, unlike the rest of the room, which was laid with tatami mats. Outside, the view was cluttered with flowers, a Zen garden laced with an unreadable pattern, and stone lanterns balanced upon long stands. My hands itched at the sight, and I hurried to my bags that had arrived in the room before I had.

Pulling out an ink brush and pad, I found myself in the familiar position of a curled spine and scrunched toes as I sat on the floor, hand moving alone as my eyes darted from place to place. It didn't take long to capture the image; neat lines, the comfortable wet smudge of black against my skin, and the usual tedious still-life replication on a background as white as snow.

'Amazing, a sumi-e painting!' Noriko exclaimed as she looked at the completed work in my hands. Taken aback, I sat in my crouched position, staring at the wonder on her face. Noticing my surprise, she bowed deeply, 'I'm very sorry for my outburst. I came to tell you that your futon has been laid. I shall excuse myself if there is nothing else that you need.'

'It's fine. Would you like it?' I offered, tearing the page from my pad.

'I could never take such lovely artwork,' she said firmly, shaking her head as if I were trying to hand her a box brimming with gold.

Insisting, I thrust the painting into her grasp, 'Don't worry about it. I've painted so many that I'm bored of them.'

'Thank you very much, Mr Usui,' her voice trembled slightly as she smiled, 'Please ring the bell on the table if you need any assistance. I shall return around six o'clock with your meal.'

'Thank you.'

Noriko's beaming expression was childish and pure as she hugged the painting to her chest. I was horrified to notice a small splatter of ink dye her blue obi black as she departed. I retired into the soft embrace of the futon, fighting to find comfort on the tiny box-shaped pillow while missing the memory foam one in my Roppongi apartment. Drifting to sleep, I dreamt I was in the presence of Noriko in her kimono, ink smudge still visible, like an impurity forced to prove something was real. As I watched the blot spread. With desires of its own, it wriggled across her clothes from her hem to her collar and across her smooth, cream skin, leaving her dishevelled under the caress of the ink.

I bolted up in a start. The room was much darker than I remembered. Still groggy, I was bewitched by the aroma of meaty broth and began searching for the smell's origin. As I noticed the outline of a body through the thin paper door, Noriko's voice broke my disorientation.

49

'Mr Usui, your dinner has been prepared. Shall I serve you?'

My mind was numb as the blanket felt heavy and wet. Glancing beneath the sheet, I noticed my indecent, semi-bulged state. *Oh, dear God.* Flushing like a virgin, I snatched the sheets and carried them over to the futon cupboard, slamming the door shut.

'Mr Usui? Are you alright?'

Panicked, I babbled while lunging for my bag, desperate to find a pair of fresh underwear, 'Just a moment.'

It took significantly less time than it felt before I called for Noriko to enter. Upon seeing her pristine appearance and gentle gestures, my heart began to tease me with beats so loud I thought she might hear them. As she crossed the room, I caught sight of my shameful garments peeking out from my duffle. Tiptoeing over, I kicked the bag onto its side, desperately trying to hide all evidence of my crime. Noriko hadn't noticed the soft thump of my bag tipping over while setting my meal down on the low table and offered to keep me company while I ate. In no frame of mind to turn her away, I agreed; my eyes fixating on the spot of ink that stood out like a black petunia in a field of hydrangeas. The meal was pleasant, with light alcohol and inviting conversation. I hadn't realised my hunger before, but now my mouth salivated as sweet meat melted on my tongue. We chatted about the Ryokan's eight-hundred-year history and Noriko's life as a Nakai. Eventually, as the meal drew to a close, Noriko's cheeks bloomed with admiration as she once again thanked me for the painting.

I was bored of such sumi-e paintings. When I was younger, I was considered a prodigy. My ability to bring ink to life with a single stroke left me standing on the highest pedestal of the art community; exhibitions, commissions, grants, and bids left me with more money than I could possibly need, but there was nothing left to paint. Flowers, with their vitality, were easily transposed; in their wilt, they were ominous and fascinating. People were cumbersome and vain. While landscapes left me empty as I stared across a vast expanse only to analyse its worth. However, the joy Noriko found within my work was fresh, innocent, and relieving; her excitement at the simplicity was revitalising.

Watching her clear the dishes, her slender arms moving in practiced motions, I asked, 'Would you let me paint you?'

My ears burned as soon as the words left my lips. *Why did I say that?* Noriko's expression was unreadable for the longest time, leaving dread and embarrassment to bubble within me. Softly, she smiled as embarrassment of her own coloured the rest of her complexion so that it matched the alcoholic warmth in her cheeks.

'Really?'

'Of course,' I said, 'if you would let me.'

Noriko agreed to meet me the next afternoon after her chores and other responsibilities had been taken care of. After she said goodnight, I found myself snuggling into my futon, guilty about the sticky stain that hadn't completely dried. Still, after another strange dream, it grew even bigger - and my sin even more mortifying.

When Noriko arrived for our session, she seemed surprised to find the floor of my room was cluttered by thin sheets of paper and various styles of ink brushes. I asked if she wouldn't mind sitting so that her right side was illuminated by the light rushing in from the engawa, and she swiftly took her position, listening carefully to my instructions. As if possessed, it took almost no time to capture her visage on paper. From minimalistic to intricate, her likeness found itself piled in places around the room.

Almost two hours later, I placed my brush on the table and invited Noriko to admire my creations. She commented on each one as if determined to ensure every moment of my effort was accounted for. I had no intention of inspecting the art. My fascination lay in her response, her changing expressions, the glee, and the flush in her skin. Pleased by her praise, my eyes drifted down to her obi. To my disappointment, it was different from the day before and had not been marred by the accidental smudging of black. Unable to ignore the image of her wrapped in vines of ink, I found myself speaking with my eyes laid hungrily on her body.

'Could I paint you?'

'You have, beautifully.'

51

'No,' I mumbled, 'I mean, may I paint your skin?' Noriko looked at me silently, unsure whether I was being sincere or not. 'I'm sorry; I didn't mean to take you by surprise. I've been an artist for so long that even when a subject excites me, the ink and canvas begin to bore me with familiarity. I want to do justice to you, a perfect muse. Would you allow me to paint directly onto your skin?'

'I don't know,' Noriko replied, 'Mr Usui, may I give you my decision later?'

'Of course, take all the time you need.'

While answering, my tone was even and considerate; however, I could feel a longing in my fingers to rush after her with a brush in my hands and use the bristles to caress her bare neck.

The next day, Noriko said little in the morning when she delivered breakfast and even less during lunch. It wasn't until the day grew dark that she seemed to reach a conclusion.

In the warm room with its snug, bare-bones interior, the furniture melted away as Noriko's kimono slipped from the upper half of her figure, exposing her skin, revealing what was hidden beneath; a blank canvas unblemished by scars or beauty marks, the perfect tone and texture yearning the touch of my brush.

I stared. My eyes were unmoving from Noriko's naked back, shaken by every breath she took as her shoulders rose softly. Without an image in mind, I brought the tip of my utensil to the base of her spine, striking hungrily upwards as if desperately trying to mark each inch of her as my own. With each stroke, my heavy breaths fell away as the ink fondled the back of her neck, her bare arms, and the edges of her breasts. Soon, orchids sprouted in shades of grey, their leaves straining to cover as much distance as possible. Enamoured by their journey, I explored Noriko's body before meeting her steady gaze that glistened with an intense shyness. Unable to pull away, I found myself captured by her tender lips, pressing against my artwork and intertwining my body with hers. Our heavy breaths turned into moans, and my reason began to completely disappear.

'Can I continue?' I whispered.

Noriko said nothing in return but unwound the many layers of remaining fabric from her lower body, inviting me into a long night of thrill and feverish ecstasy.

When my eyes flickered open, the world was kissed by summer yellow. The white blankets were warm with sunlight, and the body pressing against my arm was golden in the morning rays. The sumi-e style painting on Noriko's skin seemed beautifully smudged, almost as though it was designed to depict the insatiable nature of the world. Rising from our futon, I admired the room, still coated in an array of memories from hours before. My phone buzzed from my backpack, glowing unnaturally through the netted pocket. Looking at the alarm, I grimaced at the reminder to check who my driver would be today as I returned to Tokyo.

The bus was set for a little after mid-day, so I spent the remaining time with Noriko, sharing sweet nothings and promises that both of us knew would only be fond memories. Once my few belongings were packed, I turned to my Nakai, who was still blissfully ruffled as she laid her kimono out in order of dressing. *God, she's breath-taking.*

'Noriko, can I take a picture of your body? The ink is stunning against your figure, and your curves inspire me. I can barely resist the urge to wash you clean and start again.'

A brilliant beam shaping her lips, Noriko said, 'Mr Usui, I would like that very much.'

Holding up my phone to capture the sight of her body enveloped in my handiwork, the front of my trousers felt tight. Taking pictures from every angle I could, I slung one bag over my shoulder and allowed Noriko to take the other. We walked side-by-side to the desk inside the main building where the elderly server stood, much like during my arrival; upon seeing us, her thin eyebrows lifted in an unreadable fashion before bowing.

'Did you have a pleasant stay, Mr Usui?'

'Yes, I did.'

'Will we soon you again soon?'

53

'That would be nice.'

Noriko stood with me while all the paperwork was completed, walking me to the entrance and fetching my shoes at the entranceway. Unable to muster a farewell, my eyes clung to hers, the grip around my bag straps growing hot.

'Have a pleasant journey, Mr Usui.'

'Yuuma, my name is Yuuma.'

'Yuuma, I hope you come back soon.'

'I'll try, Noriko.'

Smiling, I left. Not once glancing back at the Ryokan or the door that hid the stunning young woman in the kimono. My pace was quick as I left the forest, not trusting I wouldn't turn back if I slowed down even a little. I arrived at the well-maintained yet barren station as the bus, swerving as recklessly as it had just three days prior, appeared in the distance. I didn't care if it was the same crazy old man driving. Collecting my ticket, I noticed that this time the boy in the booth was awake, playing on his phone and ignoring the textbook that lay open on the same page it had been the last time I saw it. I grinned and brought out my own phone, flicking through the many photos I had taken of Noriko.

When I returned to Tokyo, my studio seemed fresh and exciting, a host of potential happiness and inspiration. Grabbing the largest piece of rice paper I could find, I plastered it to a large section of the wall. On it, I released my desires, drowning in the intoxicating scent of ink and sweat. Stepping back, my body was feverish as I stared at my work; an orchid entangled around a woman's flesh, her clothes knotted around her feet, her hair hiding her thrill.

I called my agent, still burning from satisfaction, and I used an almost unattainable phrase for the first time - 'masterpiece.'

A note from the author:

Noriko's creation stemmed from my deep love of Asia, predominantly Japan. I wanted to explore the culture while portraying its deep history in a familiar yet striking way. Playing with the intensity of eroticism within the piece, I found that hints of desire contrasted beautifully against the stark traditionalism of the setting I had chosen. I was inspired by past lessons on accentuating particular colours and objects, creating symbolism that played with the reader's perception of the theme. Being only 3000 words long, I relied heavily on my classmates' perceptions of the characters' odd, though sweet, relationship; leaving the reader wondering about the encounter from another point of view.

S. J. Milne combines mature topics and fairy tales in her work, situating the majority of her writing in the fantasy genre. Having published The Witch's Cursed Daughter, the first novel of The Myrde Chronicles, on Wattpad last year, she is currently working on the second instalment of the series.

Rose

Robyn Kerr

You are like the sun, bright and burning hot.

No.

My love, I love you, I love you more than football.

No, she'll hate that.

Your hair is smooth, like the sand in a deserted…lost city.

Jesus Christ no.

My bride, your beauty is unmatched, even by a rose.

No, no fucking roses.

You make me feel loved my bonnie lass, with your sweet wide smile.

What is wrong with me? Wide smiles aren't romantic.

'Any luck?' Lee asks, putting a cup of tea down next to me, he peers over my shoulder at a page full of crossed-off crap. 'Guess not.'

I appreciate the tea; I could do without the snigger and grin. He sits across from me at this tidy, but frankly the smallest, table known to man. I've been sat here for three hours, sat on this uncomfortable, vomit coloured, rock hard chair. Three hours! Maybe if I was at home, in my nice, comfortable leather recliner, I could do this, instead of being in my brothers dirty, unkempt studio. The paint fumes alone are giving me such headaches. He is taking this artist persona to the extreme, with his forty plants, wild hair and water fasts. He's on one now, day six of just water; he looks starving. I love my brother but he needs a shower, and this living room needs hoovering.

'Write from the heart,' he tells me, as if it's that easy.

'Great idea, thanks.' I hope he got the sarcasm.

'Don't get sarky.' Good, he did. 'Compare her to a rose, women love roses.'

'No, everyone does that bollocks.' I've been to hundreds of weddings, working as a put-upon waiter; there's always someone comparing the bride to a fucking rose.

'What about something like: My darling bride, how I love you. You are sweet like a plum. I would walk on my knees for a thousand miles for you. Across the sands of time. You, my love, are perfect to me,' he grins, looking mighty pleased with himself. Robert Burns he ain't; that was worse than my shite.

'That was utter fucking bullshit.'

'Well, you clearly can't do any better.' He stands up and storms out, slamming the door of this bedroom/living/kitchen. How did this thing cost £160k? Our house was £20k less and it's a three bedroom. Right, come on Luke, you can do this, you love Kirsty. Now you just need the words to show it.

My love.

There is no one I love more.

There is no one I like more.

No one I would rather spend my life with.

You are everything to me.

My heart and soul.

I love you.

I love your weird laugh.

I love your Golden Girls *obsession.*

I even love that you nearly kill me every time you drive.

I love you Kirsty.

More than Burns loved his rose.

Fuck, now I'm talking about a rose. Fuck it, that'll do.

'Rose' is a light-hearted look at a husband to be, striving to have the best vows for his bride. He's out of his depth, as he sits in his brother's home trying not to use the word rose. Set in Glasgow, I wanted to create an easy and relatable read for anyone planning a wedding.

Where is the Rainbow?

Robyn Kerr

'You're going the wrong way,' I tell Sparkle.

'Don't start, Cotton, this is the right way. I followed the route Vanilla told us to. We went right at the candy canes, straight past the chocolate milk waterfall, then left at the ice cream volcano,' she replies. For a unicorn studying happinesses, she's being testy. Her purple coat is flaring. Clearly, Blue Floss Academy isn't getting the job done.

'Then where is the fucking rainbow?' I demand. 'We should see the fucking rainbow by now.'

'We will, we're on track,' she assures me.

Sparkle is my older cousin. This is our first task together and it will be our last. Her family live on the other side of Bubble Land, in Maple Puddle. Mum says they think they are better than us, 'cause we live in Button Slush. Button Slush isn't the nicest, it's very wet and sticky. I don't know if Sparkle does or doesn't think she's better than me, but I do know that she can't admit when she's wrong.

'Sparkle, this was meant to take three years. It's been forty-five.' I have a right to have doubts.

'It's taking longer because of you. You just had to stop at Glitter Land for a new horn, which you didn't need.'

'Of course, I needed it, my old one was completely glitter-less and sparkle-less.' It was - *and* three hundred years old. A young gal like myself needs to feel pretty.

'Well, that added on at least ten years,' she spits back at me. 'Don't forget who is leading this magical task.'

Forty years I've had to put up with her. Forty years flying side by side. She's starting to really get on my tail dust now. I want a pay rise.

'I'm going to call him,' I threaten.

'No, you are not,' she warns.

'I want to know how much longer to the rainbow.'

'We're close.'

'You don't know that.'

'Yes, I do,' she says confidently.

'Swear on your tail,' I challenge her. She loves her shitty gold tail.

'We're close,' she replies, not swearing on her tail. The lying glitterball.

I should never have agreed to this trip. My mother was all, 'You don't have any other magic going on.' I should have lied, said I was hunting lions or teaching elves how to fly. Maybe I should do more charity work. She wouldn't have checked; mum's too busy pissing rain over Scotland every day, although they don't seem to appreciate it very much, considering how much they complain. We do it out of love; we want them to look pretty, not dull and grey like England.

'How many more years? Tell me the truth,' I warn.

'I don't know for sure; I would say two, maybe four. It'll be worth it when we get there.'

'Will it, though?'

'Yes, you're young, you've never seen the magic key first hand. It will change your life, it's so shiny.'

I don't care how shiny it is, to be honest. I want to go home, float in my own gummy bear and rewatch *Russia: The Early Years*. Before they went all batshit crazy. Is that too much for a pink candy unicorn to ask for?

'Did you hear about Gold?' she asks, diverting my attention.

'That ice lolly slut from Divine Alley?'

'Yeah, apparently she's seeing Buttonhole.'

'Buttonhole? Ew, he's howling. His brother, on the other hand - I've never seen a horn that big,' I grin.

'Oh my god, I know. Silk is stunning. His mane makes my three hearts do back flips.'

'Same.'

I won't tell her that me and Silk did the unholy behind the lemon hill. Or that he was sensational. I'll need to float over there when we get back.

'Shit,' she sighs.

'What?'

'Don't get mad.'

'What?'

'We've gone the wrong way.'

Fucking stupid purple bitch.

Sixty years later…

'Ok, it is really shiny,' I admit.

'Right!'

A note from the author:

Set in the sky above Scotland, we follow two young unicorns, in their search for the shiny key. With the theme of writing from Scotland, I wanted to showcase our sharp wit, terrible weather and our ability to complain. It's aimed towards adults looking for a funny and light-hearted read.

Voices

Megan McLaughlin

Sometimes I envy those people who lost their mothers when they were born or as toddlers. It's an awful thing to lose a parent at any age, but the aftermath of that loss is worse. Forgetting your mother's voice because you didn't have enough time to memorise it - it just doesn't get harder than that.

I hate forgetting voices.

Some voices stick with you through the years. They're distinctive in their tone, or in my case, I became so obsessed with some crushes that I still have their voice committed to memory. But some voices, important voices, they don't stick like that.

My mum's voice never stuck like that.

Sometimes the most special things in life are the things we forget about because they're so mundane. We think they'll be in our lives forever, a constant by our side.

And then they aren't.

When you're not even a teenager yet, why would you commit your parent's voice to memory? It's a silly thing to do, isn't it? At eleven, you take for granted that your parent will be there always. They'll help you grow up, go to high school. A whole future of weddings and grandkids that kids never think they'll have to face alone.

That's what I thought I knew. But everything changed too quickly.

I do remember the cold of that night, out on the town in Glasgow on the last day of 2011. It was wet; so frigid that my fingers were numb in the sleeves of my anorak. Mum had been scouring shops all day, buying rings she'd never get to put on her fingers and watches she'd never see gleam on her wrist. Jewellery shops were her best friend and even better if they were cheap.

She was a slave to a bargain, one genetic trait I still carry today.

That night as the bells tolled, we cheered 2012 into existence with a glass of non-alcoholic shandy. We couldn't have known what would happen nine days later.

Her health ebbed away in a torturous timeline crafted by the reaper, and suddenly I was waking up in the early morning for school to her cries of pain. Her desperate pleas for someone to save her from the carpet she'd fallen onto in the middle of the night. Her voice raw from calling for my dad since she had awoken, him being asleep in the separate bedroom where he'd been since she broke her collarbone a year before.

He didn't hear her, and my mum lay in a state of cold and pain for hours before I awoke and came to her rescue. But I was only eleven and no help at all, so after rousing my dad awake and being told to get ready for school and 'just don't give me any backchat, be quiet and get dressed,' I had no choice.

I dressed and had cereal, watching some stupid episode of some stupid Disney Channel show, and then the lights came outside. Blue and blinding on alert.

I never spoke to her again, her last words a desperate plea for me to get my dad so he could phone the ambulance and save her life. After all, what use would I be when I had to get to school soon? She didn't want me to know what was going to happen, or maybe she hadn't figured it out yet herself. The next time I faced my mum, only a few hours later, she was a dead body on a cold bed under the ground floor of Inverclyde Royal. Her lips blue. Her face pale.

That black chasm of grief consumed me for weeks afterwards. It took me out of my body, forcing me to watch alone in my head as her coffin was rolled out the back of the crematorium. Tears I could barely feel tracked down my face as the finality of everything changing hit me. She was gone. No longer a concrete feature in my life, her voice was going to fade from memory.

A note from the author:

'Landfall' was born from many inspirations, from the pandemic to my favourite medical drama, but the primary concept of the asteroid hitting the planet came from watching the movie Don't Look Up. I wanted to create a story with all the intensity of an apocalyptic scenario, but which still kept an element of comedy and magnified a day in the life of survivors after the impact rather than the panic of waiting for the impact – which I feel is an overdone trope in Hollywood. Apocalypses are a landscape I feel comfortable and proud writing in so it made sense to put this piece into the anthology.

Voices, however, came from an exercise in class about sounds and a fleeting thought I had about my mum's voice. It shows a duality in my writing I didn't know existed and I'm happy I get to show the range of emotion that I was feeling at the time of my mother's death in a creative manner.

Megan McLaughlin studied Creative Writing BA (Hons) at the University of the Highlands and Islands 2019-23. She was a 2017 member of the 'What's Your Story?' writing program run by Scottish Book Trust and works as an intern for Stairwell Books in Edinburgh for their independent book fair each year. Additionally, she is currently working on creating a podcast about mythological creatures, and her piece about the Glencoe Massacre is featured in the Clan Cameron magazine of New Zealand http://www.clancameronnz.co.nz/newsletters/december-2022-newsletter/

Instagram: @amethystaurawriting

Winter Whispers

Isla Bain

Cars chug behind me, illuminating the road ahead leading out of town. I can hear the tyres drag against the street, the gravel scrapes against the tarmac with a muffled screech as the wheels clunk down into the snowy potholes.

My boots slide on the pavement. The dampness that fell upon the snow has now turned to ice. I grab onto the wall on the bridge, cringing as the wet moss slides underneath my nails and my palm stings as it meets stone, bare against more frost. I steady myself before heading over the final few steps off the bridge, through the thick mist of the early morning shadows, and towards my car.

Driving back across the bridge, towards the *Thank you for visiting Thurso sign* that marks the outskirts of the town, the sharp clang of salt from the gritters that pass by rains down and bangs against the sides of my car. 'Poor car,' I think aloud as I turn the music up, settling in for my forty-minute drive to my first patient's house. Only for it to be interrupted a second later by my phone ringing.

'Hello?' I croak out through my cold and achy morning voice.

'Rebecca? Where are you?' Andrew's voice blares through the speaker in my car.

'How are you so awake this early? You don't have work today.' Reaching for my coffee cup after twisting the volume dial down a bit, I'm now steering with only one hand.

'It doesn't matter. Have you started out on your rounds yet?'

'Yup,' I try to focus on my driving, 'same as I do every morning at half five.' As much as I know the road out to the estate, there are always tractors and lorries that appear out of the shadows of the rural tracks.

'Rebecca, are you crazy? It's been snowing all night, and it's freezing now into ice. It's not safe!'

I puff out a laugh, rolling my eyes at him. Such a drama queen.

'I do this route every day and have done for years. I know what I'm doing.' Just as the last syllable slips off my tongue, the wheels skid on the snow, scuffing the thick white into my side windows and throwing the car into a sharp left turn. I gasp and freeze, hovering my feet over the brake and accelerator, unsure which to go for. The steering fights against me. The vehicle still skids, but I gently press into the clutch and then the brake, easing it into a gentle stop at the side of the road but facing away from it.

'Oh my gosh, Rebecca? Rebecca, are you okay? What just happened?' The alarm in Andrew's voice sends even more blood to my brain; my whole body shakes as I pull the car out of gear and put on the handbrake, switching off the ignition, before putting both hands on my chest. My booming heart slams against my skin.

'I'm fine. I'm fine. Don't worry,' I swallow hard, 'Just a little skid.'

'How far out of town are you?' he doesn't wait for a response, 'Just turn round and go home. One day won't hurt your patients. They'll understand.' I can hear the shake in his throat as his voice cracks.

'No, it's fine, Andrew; I'm only two minutes from the first one's home.' That's a lie, but he doesn't need to know that.

'Okay, but please message when you get there and check in with your work in case they've called a snow day. It's going to be an absolute blind snowstorm tonight.' There's an echo of the crackling fire in the background of his call. I think of him wrapped up on our sofa in warm fluffy blankets, sipping on coffee, book in hand. I think of how much I'd rather be there too, tucked under his arm.

'Okay sweetie, I promise.' I can't hide the smile in my voice at the gentle image in my head, calming my heart rate down after the skid.

'Be safe. I love you.' The call cuts off before I reply, but I whisper it anyway as my music returns to the speakers.

'I love you too.'

I know I need to get the car back on the road and keep going. The more I sit and stare at the white cloud of road ahead, the less I want to drive on it.

I switch on the ignition with a trembling hand, my glasses steaming up with the fog of my deep breaths. Quickly getting into gear before gently releasing the handbrake. Inching forward with the most minor force onto the throttle pedal. I pull the steering back out of the wedge of snow it created during the slip, teasing it out of the track as slow and controlled as possible. The tyres give a brief resistance. Hesitating on the snow tracks for a few moments before giving in. Turning their trail. Finally gliding back onto the road.

The minutes pass faster than my brain (or car) can keep up with, and I know I will be late for my first visit, but it can't be helped. So long as I make it there, that's the main thing. The road feels heavy and tiresome as the car trudges through it. I experiment with the lights trying to stop the hypnotising snowfall that never ceases to distract me.

Main beam.

Dipped lights.

Main beam.

Dipped.

Main beam.

It doesn't make a difference. The main beam illuminates the road (or what's left of it, at least) but creates a tantalising maze of snowfalls that steals my attention. My eyes are dragged into the centre of the falling snow, hypnotised by the constant swirl of flakes. My grip loosening on the wheel as my attention falters.

My subconscious takes over as I shift my slippery shoes around on the foot pedals. Turning around on them, I move the pressure off from the throttle pedal just for a split second, still entranced by the snowflakes dancing, drifting, and lifting in the spotlights ahead of me.

Until BAM! The tyres roll out of the tracks, slamming against the thick, rugged borders of snow, skidding against the ice. I can feel the wheels spinning rapidly. Turning, but with no control. Rotating upon the surface but getting no traction or power to fight against the white layers and return to the course.

My palms are instantly moist, and tears rush to my eyes, further impairing my vision. My heart bashes against my ribcage at the same pace as the wheels of my car do in the mounds of snow. My knuckles tighten around the wheel, the material of my scrubs tightening around my biceps as I battle to control the direction. But to no avail. The back end of the car swings out. I can see the rusted black and silver railing on the verge of the road, coming closer and closer. But something else is needed. No matter what, I push on the pedals; the car is rendered useless; the snow takes over, leaving me powerless.

One last desperate attempt to encourage the brakes to kick in and stop doesn't work. The car rattles as it thumps and trundles up over the curb before smashing into the railing, tearing it out of the ground. The car feels heavy and laden as the railing drags along, must be stuck around the bumper of my car; I hear something crumple and shatter and the clanging of what I can only presume is the engine. I take a deep breath, knowing what lies beyond that railing. Grip tightening, I become paralysed in my seat as the car zips down the hill. The snow doesn't slow me down as the car plumages over the frosty grass of the field. Still frozen in my seat, I can only watch as a giant oak tree comes into view, rolling straight into our path. It stands tough and tall, and I brace for impact with it. My breath is trapped in my throat, my heart booming through my head until I'm left with a ringing in my ears and a white static vibration. The car plumets into the tree. Metal crunches and the oak snaps and my vision is blocked by the thick, heavy white airbag as it bursts out of the dashboard.

It's still. Everything stopped. The car isn't moving. My body is weak, and I'm slumped over the now-deflated airbag. There's a muffled rumbling and creaking sound, but it's dimmed and muted. A flickering yellow in the corner of my vision and warmth seeped over my prickled, goose-bumped skin. Until that flicker of light disappears, a dark shadow takes over my view, and my lungs pull out a deep, shaking breath.

Leaving me in darkness.

Though it was the beginning of summer, there was still a whisper of the stinging spring gales. I pulled my trench coat tighter around my shoulders. I swung my book-filled backpack over my shoulder and continued walking home from the pub where I had gotten a part-time gig.

Usually, weeknights were quiet nights as far as customers went, but that night was different. I ran a finger along the cash that was stuffed into my pocket. I had taken advantage of the busy hustle and bustle and helped myself to a couple of twenties from the till. Even then, I had managed to charm the boss into gifting me a bottle of red "for my troubles," as he liked to call it.

I remember stumbling, mumbling, and grumbling to myself as I staggered through the apartment lobby doors. I had swung them open with one hand and used the other to keep a tight clasp around the neck of the then half-empty bottle of red.

Step after step, my six-inch violation of the work dress code heels rubbed like sandpaper against my feet as I trudged up the stairs. I took another swig as I climbed the stairs; I heard footsteps echo around the stairwell out of nowhere. The sound getting louder and louder, until I was faced with a tall, muscular bloke taking up a large portion of the hallway. He watched as I fought against each step. I ignored him, continuing my struggle.

'You just going to ignore me then?' He chuckled and swung an arm under my shoulders.

A vague strike of recognition hit me. A strand of his curly blonde hair fell over his face when he pushed against my body, forcing me to walk faster up the steps.

'Do I know you?' I mumbled sarcastically in an attempt to flirt. I remember fondling through my pockets to find my cigarettes.

'You're such a mess, Rebecca. ' His grip tightened as he huffed and puffed in frustration.

69

I tried to turn around but stumbled. I reached out for the stairwell's banister to save myself, but Cole was quicker as he jumped down a few stairs to steady me.

'Of course, you would think that.' Inches away from my face. I fired a sarcastic toothy grin in his direction.

'I haven't seen or heard from you in days, Cole! You're supposed to be my boyfriend?!' I started yelling at that point. My lungs were wheezing in between sobs.

'Consider yourself lucky I'm even here at all! I don't need you, remember.'

I flung the cigarette end out of my hand and brought the bottle to my lips as he continued.

'You need me, Rebecca! Not the other way around.' He hissed as he pushed my shoulder towards my apartment door.

I poured out the last of the bottle into my mouth as it trickled down my throat. I felt the toxins rush to my head, which rendered me, once again, absent on absinthe.

I wake up with a startle, trying to jump up but trapped between the slanted chair and the crushed dashboard. I don't get far, and even then, it sends agony up my spine. My mouth is dry, course and scratchy from the back of my throat to the edge of my lips. Running my tongue over my lips to bring back some moisture, I realise how cold they are.

There's a dull ringing in my head. I slowly peel my eyes open, wincing at the bright light that pours in, shining right through my head with a high-pitched static dance around my brain.

Rebecca

Blowing the fluff of my bunched-up scarf away from my chin, trying to haul myself back upright, I feel the hot, sticky, thick fluid trickling down my head. A crimson trail appears in my peripherals, pouring a slow glop down my cheek towards my chin. Then it comes back to me.

The dark.

Rebecca

The snowflakes.

Rebecca

The lights.

Rebecca

The skidding.

Rebecca

And then the crash.

Rebecca

'What?!' I yell out, my voice tearing my vocal cords and burning my lungs as it puffs out the warm breath into the ice-cold air.

Can you speak to me?

I don't move. Stilling my breathing as much as possible and hovering my frozen blue hands in place. There's no way. I see slight movement beyond the blood trail on my cheek. It is slight. Almost invisible. But it's there. Movement. Company. A person.

'Cole?' I'm trembling.

Honestly, sweetheart, what a state you've gotten yourself in.

I know it's him. That melodic, welcoming, and confident voice is unmistakable. I swallow the lump in my throat and slowly turn to the passenger side. The car is still. The engine must have given out when I was passed out, but a grey haze of cloud seeps in through the vents across the dashboard.

That voice. It's been so long since I heard that voice; I almost forgot it. It triggers immediate tears to stream down my face. Warmth spreads from my stomach, butterflies carrying it from my stomach to my head.

'Cole!' I sob, forcing myself to turn, contorting my body as much as my pain tolerance allows.

It's the blonde hair I notice first. Platinum curls cascaded down the top of his head. A thick black woollen duffle jacket covered his slight frame. I can't see his face yet, needing to turn my body around more but stuck between the crumpled dash, steering wheel digging into my stomach, tangled in the deflated airbag. I give a gentle twist but retreat when it sends shooting stabs from the bottom of my spine to my skull.

Hush, my sweetheart. Don't strain yourself.

An icy hand pushes against my head, lulling it back into the headrest before swiping a finger against my wound, smudging it. But I can see him now. The big thick-rimmed glasses that he never changed, circling the bright cerulean orbs.

I let out another sob. Those eyes. So many memories and emotions come rushing through my brain. It feels like forever since I've seen those eyes.

I woke up with a groan and peered through the thick fake lashes stuck to my eyelids, I dug my sharp acrylics into the frayed material and tried to pull myself up, but nausea hit.

'Morning, Rebecca.' That cheery voice rang through the empty room; his words were dripped in fake concern but rang out like condescension in my head. His eyes were puffy, rimmed in red, and covered in a thin layer of tears.

I grunted at him, unable to form words against my sandpaper throat and wet mouth. Must have drunk a lot more than I realised that night. I slipped a shaking hand down the crease of the couch before pulling out my pack of cigarettes. I balanced it between my lips, smudging the white of the cigarette in my cheap red stain as I fumbled for a lighter. Left pocket. Right pocket. Floor.

'Here,' He waved a small flame under my nose. He didn't smoke, I didn't know why he had a lighter, but I didn't care to ask. I took a long drag before blowing the smoke into the room's cold.

'Thanks.'

My stomach churned. I leant across the arm of the couch and, before I could comprehend what was happening, threw up onto the carpet. I had left behind the distinctive acidic bile trapped inside my mouth; it stuck to my tongue and plastered onto my teeth. I stubbed out the cigarette and threw it onto the table as another wave of fatigue hit, so I shuffled back to lie down, snuggling my neck into my shoulders against the harsh cold air of the apartment.

'I'm so sorry, Rebecca,' he sniffled. I peeled my damp, but crusted eyelids open to look at him; I fired him a quick nod before sitting up and inviting him in for a cuddle. It was as if I was on autopilot. So used to the same circle of emotions.

He yells. I cry. He sleeps. I stay silent. He yells again. Then he cries. Then I forgive him.

He sat down and pulled me into a tight embrace. He whispered how much he loved me into my ear in between sobs while he squeezed his arms around me; his grip never faltered.

'I've got to go to work in a minute. Be ready for me when I get home tonight, and I'll take you out someplace nice.' He squeezed my waist. I giggled and smiled up at him.

'But sober up before then. I'm not being seen with a drunk again.' His voice had turned grave.

I nodded. 'Of course. Sorry Cole,' I whispered.

'I haven't seen you in so long, Cole. Almost five years.' My tears warm up my cheeks as they fall thick and fast.

Don't cry.

He smiles at me, still swiping at the leaking wound, fussing with my hair. I can't stop crying, though. Just looking at him. Getting to see him. There's so much to say, so much that he's missed.

Don't cry.

He moves both hands to cradle my face. Staring right into my eyes. But he changes. As my tears pool against his thumbs on my cheeks, his eyes harden, and his smile fades.

I said,

His hands tighten. Slowly, he just pressed his palm firmer into my frozen skin.

Don't cry.

His voice booms. Banging against the sides of the car walls, vibrating off my body, making my bones quake. He digs his nails in properly now, fingers tightening, nails slicing through my flesh.

'Ow, Ow! Okay, I've stopped!' I take deep gulping breaths in, as if I can suck up and reabsorb the already fallen tears.

Smoke floats across the dashboard and over me, fogging my vision. It snakes up in strands, wrapping itself around Cole's arms, then pulling my ex's hands away as it drifts past us. His eyes scrunch at the corners, narrowing with a furrowed brow before the hard, cold blue stare disappears in the fog.

The indents of where his hands were on my cheeks burn as I run a blue fingertip over the ghost of his touch. Another wave of smoke washes over me. I close my eyes to block out the sting of it on my swollen, red eyes. My chest racks with a dry, silent sob. I can feel myself drifting towards unconsciousness as his voice rings through my mind. *Don't cry.*

There was a significant level of darkness already hanging over the sky. I was driving home. My sinuses were blocked and achy as I turned my head before approaching the junction. I remember the seatbelt alert sounding from the car; the stack of books wobbled on the passenger seat as I pulled up to the house. My phone was vibrating in the cupholder. Another phone call to add to the text messages that had been piling up since I left work. I popped my seatbelt, pulled the handbrake, pushed the car out of gear, and turned off the ignition. But I couldn't move. I was staring at the house. The black-painted wooden fence. The big white stone walls. The 'welcome' sign that hung before the front door mocked me with its tantalising font and warm flower decorations. I remember the pain shooting from my sinuses up to my head as I relax into the seat, letting my arms hang and my tears well up in my eyes.

My home. That building was my home. I should have been eager to get in, greet everyone and let them know about how my day was. But I wasn't. But I couldn't.

'Why were you sitting in the car for so long?' he barked as soon as I got through the door. I took a few steps backwards but remained silent.

'Is our house not good enough for you?' He stalked forward. 'You think you are so much better than us, don't you?' A smirk was plastered across his lips. I shook my head. My eyebrows had risen in innocence. I had lifted both hands up in surrender, too.

'Well, why not then? You make us all feel like shit, you know that, right?' he spat out before he headed back through the house.

I just stood there. Staring into space, thinking.

I'm beginning to feel like shit too.

You look sad. Aren't you happy to see me?

He has turned away from me, facing the front window, hands folded neatly on his lap, looking quite comfortable and settled. I can see my breath in front of me, adding to the ever-growing levels of fog within the car. I try to wiggle my toes within my boots, but I can't feel them. The morning is beginning to set in, and there are tufts of sunlight trying to seep through, but the sky is still dull. The clock usually attached to my front heating vent is gone, so I'm still determining the time.

'Of course, I am, Cole.' I twist my head; it's a bit more comfortable to move around now. I brush my cheek against the collar of my coat, sending a burning, twitching sting across my face.

Well, you certainly don't seem happy. No wonder you can't keep a long-term relationship or friendships if that's how you treat people.

I scoff under my breath, turning away from him.

'I'm sorry, I am happy to see you,' I smile as I think about how extraordinary it is that he's here. I let my train of thought slip and start to question why he's here or even how, but that thought stops me in my tracks. My heartbeat rises, and my head suddenly gets heavy on my shoulders.

Took you long enough. There's a smirk in his voice, but it's accompanied by concern and caution, as though he knew what was happening but didn't know how to fix it, so he was waiting until I figured it out for myself.

I look at him again. He does have a white glow surrounding him, and his figure is generally patchy, as though he's been blurred at the lines of his body. My heart sinks. My mouth dries. And my brain fills with panic as it starts to drown in anxiety.

'Wh-hat-t-s-s…' I struggle to control the word. My mouth twists out of shape as though my lips are trying to catch up with the sounds my throat makes.

'Ha-a-pp-en-n-i-n-n-g-g?' My tongue feels heavy and sticky as it slogs around the words. I can't understand my own words as I hear them; they are just contorting together in a drunken-like slur.

You know what's happening. It's minus ten degrees, and you've been here for hours.

Great. Hypothermia. That's why my ex is here. Because he's not really here. He's not here.

I look towards the front windscreen as the light pours through the broken branches and clumps of snow. But it buzzes. The whole front dashboard vibrates as though the engine has decided to come back to life. But it hadn't. The entire car was buzzing. I lift a gentle hand up towards my face, but it is too numb to control the fingers. I just watch as it shakes uncontrollably. Then it hits me. The car isn't vibrating at all. In fact, everything is still apart from the dancing snow that trickles outside and me, whose body seems to be shaking beyond my control.

Sweetheart, you need to try and get out of here.

I ignore him. That word 'sweetheart' stings as it echoes in the car. No! I am a college-educated person; I have the brain capacity to know what I can and can't do. And one thing I cannot do right now is get out of this car.

But you could try.

I don't even turn my head to acknowledge him, giving him the blatant silent treatment. If I don't accept him, then I'll trick my brain out of this hallucination it has created.

No, it won't.

'Get… out of…. My…. head!' I slur, as I try to slam my hands down onto the wheel in frustration but miss and end up throwing my arm forward and hitting my hands on the cracked windscreen. A rough and shaky cry escapes my throat as I gasp out. My lips cracked.

Rebecca, I am here because you want me to be. It was YOUR mind that brought me here. You can't turn the blame onto me this time.

'This time'. As if there was ever a time where he took ownership of his wrongs. It was always me who had to apologise. Always me who had to make amends. 'Say sorry,' 'Say sorry to your brother and sister,' 'Say sorry to your friends,' 'Say sorry to *my* friends who already hate you.' I never got an apology, even if I really wanted one.

Even if I really needed one.

How's that boyfriend of yours, anyway?

'Huh?' My question fogs ahead of me.

Your Boyfriend, Andrew? Isn't it?

'Yeah…' I feel as though I'm swimming through tar to try and comprehend what he's saying, searching through a pile of cotton balls to try and grasp a strand of remembrance, '…Yeah…maybe.'

Ahhh…there it is.

He sniggers in between his tsk's of disapproval.

'There's what?' I snap back; I no longer have the time or energy for these mind games.

Can't remember your own boyfriend's name? Either he's not making the impression you think he is, or you're slipping into the clutches of hypothermia.

He's right. This is getting out of hand. Memory loss. I try again to wiggle my toes or move my legs even slightly. But I can't even see them from the crumpled dash, deflated airbag, and steering wheel still embedded into my stomach.

Morning sunlight poured through the kaleidoscopic stained windows and cast vibrant beams of colour that projected through the old church hall, a rainbow sheet laid atop the congregation as they welcomed the priest's telling's with open ears. While they gripped every syllable uttered from the Christian man's mouth, I felt a pinch on my hand as I rested on my knees.

My attention was brought back to the cloaked old minister as he clucked his book down on the pedestal and croaked out the passage, 'Lead me by your truth and teach me, for you are the God who saves me. All day long I put my hope in you - Psalm 23'.

There was another pinch on my hand as I followed the trail of where the pain was coming from, only I was met with those clenched, angry eyes that I knew all too well. I could feel his pent-up frustration as it seeped out of his gaze. I'm in for it when I get home, I thought, dreading having to leave this pew.

God had always been a figure of hope for me, and now I clung to him like my last breath.

Enough is enough. I can't sit here helpless anymore, or I will die. Here. In a random field. In the middle of a snowstorm. In my work scrubs. Alone.

Well. Alone aside from the hallucination of Cole, who is hardly even sitting in the passenger seat anymore. He's now perched on the edge, staring at me. Emotionless.

'What?' I snap again, still trying to wiggle my legs out from being trapped so I can escape. I scratch my hand for a bit, relieving an itch before it spreads to my neck.

Itchy?

'A wee bit,' I scowl at him, and he just stares at me with that dumb smirk. This itch starts to travel again, moving down my neck, back, and arms. Ouch.

'What is...?' I position my hands as far in front as possible, shocked at the small red lumps littering my pale, sweating skin. As if seeing was acknowledging, suddenly I'm burning, and the itches crawl underneath my skin over my whole body.

I clench my fists. Tears burning trails.

I thump my head back against the headrest; it sends waves of prickles through my brain, like casting a sheet of pins and needles over my body. I look towards Cole. His body was still perched, frozen, and unmoving, just staring at me.

My mouth dries, and my tongue swells as I try to form a question, but I can't. I just raise my eyebrows at him and hope he gets it. He clearly does as he leans toward me. Moving in a blur of motion, I feel his hands grip the sides of my face, surprisingly warm as I lean into them. Falling back into that comfort. But I freeze. Pull back slightly before he tightens his grip to stop me.

I've missed you so much, you know.

I hear his words ring through the car, echoing off the crumpled walls and into my mind. But I don't feel them. His words feel empty and cold. And it hits me.

'I haven't,' I shake my head. My mind flashes with images of Andrew and I, our first date. First kiss. First time meeting his family. His smile. His laugh. The feeling of his hand in mine and being able to lean on him when I'm feeling weak.

'I haven't missed you, Cole. And I don't think I ever will.' A big smile takes over my face, pushing Cole's hands off me. I try to hold it in, but a puff of joyful laughter emerges. But Cole doesn't look angry. He doesn't have his usual enraged eyes or the crease between his brows.

He just nods. Silently. Gently. Before he's gone. Vanished into the snowfall outside. Gone with the harsh breeze that rattles through the car.

I close my eyes, still laughing to myself.

*

'She will be okay, though, Andrew. It'll take a little recovery time, with plenty of rest and support, but she will be fine.'

'I just want her to be okay,' His voice is heavy with tears, crackling with a frog in his throat and a knot in his breath. I can feel his clammy palm in mine, so I give it as hard a squeeze as I can muster.

I peel my eyes apart and smile at his worried face. And all the troubles and memories of Cole disappear. Because of Andrew. He is my person. Holding my hand, ready to fix a heart that he didn't break.

A note from the author:

My short story 'Winter Whispers' is a piece of fiction that's based around the challenges of relationships and how even though the troubling ones might have ended, they can still influence our daily lives; however, it is not about what has happened in our past, it's about how we can heal, grow, and learn from it. I have always gravitated towards eerie and mysterious writing littered with enigma throughout. However, I wanted to try and create a piece that had authentic morals and life experiences throughout. I wanted to embody the difficulty of having to face your past and deal with it, so I put Rebecca in a hostage situation, in this case, the frost, where she had no other choice but to deal with it. While *Winter Whispers* isn't a personal reflection, I hope the reader can take away the importance of coping with your feelings face to face.

It's Not What It Looks Like

Elle Paterson

He looked from the Sat Nav to the house, then back again. Surely this couldn't be right? When his boss at the Herald had told him he had an interview with world renowned criminal forensic psychologist, Doctor Katherine Kershaw, he hadn't expected to find her in a quiet residential neighbourhood in Inverness.

He'd suggested they interview over lunch at one of the posh hotels in town, on the Herald's expense account, but instead, she'd insisted that he come to her home, telling him it would be more comfortable for her. He would usually have a photographer with him, but apparently that, too, would make her 'uncomfortable'. He suspected she might be a bit of a diva.

But he didn't complain. This could be the exclusive that could lead to better things for him, so he was determined to make the most of the opportunity. Doctor Kershaw had virtually become a recluse, rarely appearing in public or giving interview. Not like the old days when she'd be doing press conferences after high-profile arrests, or popping up on chat shows to promote her latest book on the psychology of killers. He'd heard that the FBI sometimes came all the way from America to consult with her. He imagined the chaos at Inverness's small airport when they tried to get their guns through security.

He grabbed his Dictaphone and exited the car. Before he was even halfway along the path, the front door was wrenched open to reveal a middle-aged, overweight woman in scruffy leggings and old, worn slippers. She didn't speak, just studied him intently as she lit up a cigarette. He gave her his most professional smile.

'Hi there. I'm Craig Bain. I'm here to interview Doctor Kershaw.'

The woman didn't answer. Just stared at him through a cloud of smoke before gesturing over her shoulder with her thumb.

'Oh, okay.'

Charming! Whoever she was, she was very rude.

81

He waited expectantly for her to move aside, but she stood there, silently puffing away, never taking her eyes off him. Since she was blocking half the doorway, he was forced to squeeze awkwardly past her into the foyer of the large house. An open door to his left led into a cosy sitting room.

'Would you like a tea or coffee before you start?' Her gravelly voice sounded muffled from the hallway.

'Coffee would be lovely, thank you. Just milk.'

He took the opportunity to study the room.

Photos in mismatched frames covered every inch of the wall above the cold fireplace. Toddlers, school uniforms, and teenage embarrassments looked down at him in remorseless succession. Further along the wall, the pictures became wedding photos, the subjects still easily identifiable by their bright red hair and broad smiles. He couldn't see any photos of his host. Curiouser and curiouser.

Creations such as a toilet roll tube glued to a coaster with a child's scrawling of 'World's Best Mum' jostled for space alongside a selection of trophies for 'Player of the Year' or 'Most Promising Ballerina' on a nearby bookcase. The layer of dust on these suggested they were not recent acquisitions. They seemed out of place amongst the titles on the equally dusty bookshelf that read like a who's who of criminal profiling, some penned by Katherine Kershaw.

The rude woman returned and passed him a mug, staring as she circled him like prey. He felt as though he were about to be consumed by her. He wasn't sure if he should make small talk or not, but then she surprised him by throwing herself in the big armchair by the fire. Was she there to take notes?

Perching on the couch, he took a mouthful from the mug she handed him, almost choking on the undrinkable, strong tea. His face screwed up in disgust. Tea! And there were about six sugars in there. Without saying a word, he searched for a space on the cluttered coffee table amongst the bits of litter and old newspapers, anywhere he could set the dreadful thing down. Not finding somewhere, he utilized a frayed issue of Bella magazine.

Just as he brought out his recorder to prepare for the interview, a large, black cat jumped down from the top of a unit onto the couch beside him. Startled, he pulled away, pursing his lips.

'Ari, get out of it,' the woman barked at the creature. The cat gave an unimpressed lick of its paw before sauntering off at its own pace. 'Sorry.' She openly smirked at his discomfort. 'That animal has a mind of its own.'

He smiled back. 'Ari, as in Aristotle?'

'No. Ari as in Ariana Grande. Are you ready yet?'

He nodded. He watched the door expectantly for the doctor to arrive. Perhaps she liked to make a grand entrance.

'Ask away.'

It took a moment for the horror to dawn on him. This was Doctor Kershaw he was sitting with. Surely that couldn't be right? Doctor Kershaw was a woman of great intelligence and formidable standing in the world of forensics. She didn't dress like a lumpy housewife or serve her guests builders tea.

To cover his embarrassment and regain his professionalism, he clicked into interview mode.

'So, Doctor Kershaw, may I call you Katherine?'

'Absolutely not,' she scowled at him. 'It's Doctor Kershaw.'

Wrong footed, he spluttered to apologise.

'I meant no disrespect Doctor Kershaw. Okay, so, err, Doctor Kershaw, can you tell me how you first became involved in your most notorious case, the case of the Saturday Strangler?'

She sighed and rolled her eyes. She didn't answer, just stared without saying a word until, to ease the discomfort, he spoke again, breaking the awkward silence.

'Did you approach the police about becoming invol....'

83

'Do you not like cats?'

The interruption was sharp. Rude and abrupt. He shook his head, indicating he didn't.

'What about dogs?'

He considered this for a few seconds.

'Yes, I guess I like dogs.'

She nodded, as though he had passed some test. With a gesture of her hand, she indicated he should continue with his questions.

'So, Doctor Kershaw, how did you first become involved in the case of the Saturday Strangler?'

'Well now, that was an interesting case.' She sat back in her chair sipping her tea, seemingly lost in thought. 'You know, I never....' She trailed off. 'I haven't offered you cake!'

She jumped up and rushed out of the room, pulling her worn blue cardigan around her expansive frame as she went. He stared after her in confusion until she returned, triumphantly brandishing a box of Mr Kipling's French Fancies. Without a word, she opened them and tipped the entire contents onto his lap.

'We don't stand on ceremony here,' she crowed. 'You don't want a plate, do you?'

He stared in confusion at the little iced cakes nestling inappropriately in his crotch. What the hell was happening here?

'Ahh no, no it's fine, thank you.'

He discreetly gathered them together, placing them awkwardly on the table alongside his tea. She watched with hooded eyes, sipping from her own mug.

'Okay so, the Strangler case,' he carried on.

'Yes, fascinating case. Do you know why his moniker was the 'Saturday Strangler'?' she asked. He nodded.

'Because he only killed on a Saturday!' she declared triumphantly.

That seemed rather obvious.

'And because he strangled his victims?'

'That too.' She looked accusingly at him, as though he had stolen her thunder. 'You're not drinking your tea.'

He was perplexed but determined to get this interview back on track. He ploughed on.

'Doctor Kershaw, can you tell us what led you to the details in your profile that enabled the police to capture him and end his reign of terror?'

'Yes, absolutely.'

His pen hovered expectantly over the blank page.

'I told them, I said, "look for a strangler who likes to kill on a Saturday."' She sat back in her chair, grinning triumphantly. 'And do you know what? They did just that. And caught him too.'

His heart sunk. He doesn't know who this woman is, but he's pretty sure she's NOT the eminent psychologist whose expertise has been sought by police departments around the world. Could this be some sort of set up by his editor, a man he was already convinced hates him? Or perhaps she was an obsessed fan of Doctor Kershaw, who saw the chance to live vicariously through her. That made more sense to him.

'*Doctor* Kershaw,' he asked, sardonically emphasising the title. 'It's rumoured that as well as lecturing at various educational institutions, you have several doctorates and a list of professional qualifications from some of the world's most prestigious universities. Is that true?'

Let's see her try to get out of that one.

She waved her hand dismissively and sipped her tea without answering. He wasn't letting her off the hook that easy, so he persevered.

'Well then, do you think I could see them?'

'Sure.'

She turned in her seat and hung over the back of it to rummage around in the depths behind it. As she did so, the back of her cardigan rode up to reveal her underwear through the thin, cheaply made leggings she was wearing. He averted his eyes in embarrassment when he noticed they had a huge split along the seam.

'I'm pretty sure this is where I left them.' Her voice sounded distorted from behind the chair.

She eventually dragged out several framed diplomas, each bearing the name 'Doctor Katherine Kershaw' with a string of letters after. He scrutinised each one, searching for signs of forgery, before placing it at his feet.

'Diplomas are all well and good,' she murmured, clutching one frame to her chest. 'But this is the one I always keep on hand, to inspire me when I feel like the world is out of balance.'

He was even more confused. He reached over and took the heavy frame she was passing him and found himself staring at a small grey kitten clinging to a rope with the motto '*Hang in There*' printed underneath.

Oh, for god's sake! Enough was enough.

'All right, that's plenty!' He leaped up to his feet, his face reddening in anger. 'I don't know who you are or what you're playing at, but this isn't funny now.' Her jaw dropped and she sat back, staring up at him dumbfounded.

'I don't understand, whatever do you mean?' Her words came out in one big rush. Behind her glasses, her eyes grew huge. His disgusted look took in the holes in her leggings, her slippered feet, the untidy ponytail of ginger hair tied back on her head.

'You're not Katherine Kershaw at all, are you?' he sneered. 'You're just some wannabe determined to waste my time!'

He gathered his things, ready to storm out. 'Just out of curiosity who are you? Her cleaner?'

At that, she gave him the sweetest smile. Her dull eyes suddenly sparkled with intelligence as she studied him intently. This time, he felt as though he had failed her test.

'Welcome to your first lesson in profiling,' she informed him. 'Where you learn to look beyond your expectations of how someone should present. Because it's only when you overcome your own preconceived notions that you can start to notice what is actually there.'

He stared at her in disbelief. Still standing, he gestured around the room.

'Was this some kind of a set up?'

She nodded enthusiastically.

'I had to shock you out of your idea of what a psychologist should look and act like. You thought you'd come to a plush office suite with an elegant receptionist and a coffee machine. Instead, you came here to meet someone so different from your expectations, you couldn't see past that. You took the dreadful tea I made you, accepted my erratic behaviour, my rudeness, because you initially believed I was an 'important person' who was smarter than you. Which is something psychopaths capitalise on to get away with their crimes.'

A slow smile crept across his face as her words sunk in. She was right, and he was embarrassed at his own stupidity.

How she was dressed, how she behaved, her god-awful tea making skills - none of that had any bearing on her ability to do her job. Yet he had dismissed her out of hand because she didn't fit the 'profile'. He'd even gone so far as to assume she was the doctor's domestic help.

He sunk back down onto the couch.

'Very clever, Doctor Kershaw.'

'Please, call me Katherine.'

'That was a nice touch by the way,' he laughed, gesturing towards the hand-crafted items on the bookcase. 'Those tatty old bits, did you fashion them from the rubbish?'

Her face turned to stone.

'My kids did actually make those.'

A note from the author:

Elle Paterson is a crime writer who likes to write different genres whenever the mood moves her. She is interested in challenging perceptions and expectations with her stories, believing writers need to keep it fresh and interesting for readers. If you enjoy this short story, then please check out more of her work on her author website www.writingpearls.co.uk

Seaweed and Roses

Ashleigh Tucker

Is it possible to love the demons?

Living within the devil that is me.

Constant battles, they linger for seasons

refusing to ever let me live free.

Praying for failure. They are relentless.

After each attack they walk hand in hand

ensuring I am on the defensive.

Forcing me to break under their command.

Down on my knees, I am begging them, 'please'.

I need them to ease, to turn and retreat.

Stop turning decades into centuries.

See it as mercy rather than defeat,

but for them I am too hard to resist.

How can I love when I barely exist?

How can I love when I barely exist

and the illness is drowning me alive?

In a war this demon needs no assist;

I am flooded without taking a dive.

Even on land I am gasping for air

as my lungs fight desperately to survive.

Wheezing and coughing, I'm very aware

it is nearly impossible to thrive.

Struggling to breathe, a chest that feels raw;

it is a lifetime of constant panic.

I am forced to live by this demon's law

everyday until I'm in a casket.

There is no blame. It is nobody's fault.

History says I was born kissed by salt.

History says I was born kissed by salt

and I can taste the seaweed on my tongue.

Coughing and spluttering is my default;

but it is not restricted to my lungs.

There's a green coating throughout my body,

sticky, it grows smothering my organs.

This demon doesn't offer a 'sorry',

to it I am easily forgotten.

Strangers turn to me, 'please die quietly.'

I can't catch my breath; I have got to leave

I don't fit into your society.

Finally. It's out my body. Breathe. Breathe.

The phlegm in the sink would have me strangled

from the seaweed, rose vines sprout, entangled.

From the seaweed rose vines sprout, entangled.

They wrap around me, thorns piercing my skin.

The vines restrain me, leaving me shackled.

I can't see a future. Is that my sin?

Every breath and moment drain's me of life,

I would rather be asleep than awake.

The thorns cut me deep, slicing like a knife.

When conscious I'm afraid that I will break.

I nap. Maybe this time I won't wake up.

Plunge into darkness. A dreamless slumber.

I open my eyes, the pains develop;

a pulsating headache makes life tougher.

How can I get up when I'm exhausted?

Paranoid, these roses have me haunted.

Paranoid, these roses have me haunted

as they drive me towards insanity.

Whispering in my ear that I'm unwanted,

so that I am their only casualty.

I have to apologise for speaking.

'I'm sorry'. I can't look you in the eyes.

Each conversation voices are shrieking,

I can't tell, what is true and what is lies?

I feel I'm vibrating internally

but on the outside, I'm completely numb.

Constant battles take a toll mentally,

I would feel at home in an asylum.

I have tried but if you didn't notice,

I can't suffocate seaweed and roses.

I can't suffocate seaweed and roses,

not without strangling myself as well.

All day and night I try not to focus

that I'm living in a crippling hell.

It's sunny outside. So I close the blind;

these roses grow sharper in the darkness.

There's wind outside. But air is hard to find

and the seaweed still tangles regardless.

Of motivation I am always drained,

without energy I can't stay awake.

This relationship is eternally strained.

I'm struggling. How much more I can take?

All I want is peace, but I am condemned.

These demons, I don't think I can love them.

These demons, I don't think I can love them.

If they disappeared, they would not be missed.

It's my body. All they bring is mayhem.

However, I could learn to coexist.

Despite the thorns and roses, I still stand.

I clear the seaweed so that I can breathe.

Refusing to acknowledge their demands

but accepting that they will never leave.

I am making 'me' a priority

to escape insanity and be free.

Cystic Fibrosis and anxiety.

Depression, fatigue, insecurities.

Constant battles, they linger for seasons;

Is it possible to love the demons?

Landfall

Megan McLaughlin

All things must end. The good, the bad, the middling. None of it is infinite, impermanence is a fact of nature. And so it tracks, using logical reasoning, that even the moral ambiguity of the human race had to end at some point too. After all, the dinosaurs had their moment in the spotlight. As it travelled towards the planet like a slow-moving bullet, fire and brimstone hurtling through space at their world and yet seeming so sedate. Just a simple light in the sky until it got too close, and Earth's gravity well brought it crashing down. They might have spotted it about a week before it hit, but with no technology to catch this flying mass funeral, what else could they do but wait for the inevitable end?

But when catastrophe has already struck, when fire and brimstone of a different calibre has already wreaked havoc on the earth, would humanity care about that light in the sky?

This question barely fazed Daphne as she drifted from her dream of existential pondering. The world of the living was quiet, so quiet she could hear her blood pound in her ears. The darkness of the sky outside met her eyes. It was still grey.

'I think it's morning, you know.'

'You can't see the sun to know if it's morning or not, Poppy.'

The arm that draped over Daphne's waist like a second blanket tightened as Poppy shifted closer to her, until their bodies were flush against each other, the older woman's chin tucking neatly into the space between Daphne's jaw and shoulder. The flowery aroma of Poppy's black hair cut through the stale air of their shared apartment as it brushed against her nose.

'I know that, but I just get that sense. And look at that, I was right.' She remarked, prompting Daphne to look towards the clock on her bedside table.

Sure enough, it was almost seven-thirty.

'I need to get up for work soon.'

'I don't think your boss will mind if you're a couple minutes late.'

Daphne laughed at that, finding the energy to turn around in her grip and give Poppy a pointed look. She couldn't feel the usual dampness of Poppy's nightwear against her arm today. It must have been a cold night.

'I think my boss needs to get up for work too.'

'My brother can handle things alone for now, Daph, I'm sure all the residents have made it in already.'

'And what if they haven't? One of the tunnels might have collapsed again and you know how easy it is to get a puncture in your suit out in the open. Or God forbid, one of them could have contracted Nova-25.'

Poppy ignored her valid points in favour of burying her face back into her pillow, letting out a sigh from deep in her lungs and keeping her eyes shut, even as Daphne sat up and stretched her arms above her head. Her back cracked to alleviate some of the pressure on her joints before she finally got out of bed, switched on the light and stood watching as Poppy retreated further into the pillow under her head.

'Poppy, I'm not kidding, we have patients to see.'

'I'm only asking for one more hour, Daph!'

Just as she argued back again, the thin black minute hand hit half past the hour and the room filled with the loud quacking of a duck. Poppy grabbed her pillow and wrapped it around her head to try and block out the incessant noise.

'Shut it off!'

'Get up for work first!'

It didn't take long for Poppy to sit up after that, launching her pillow at Daphne's head and getting out of the bed to turn off the quacking. Afterwards, she stomped to her wardrobe as if she were five years old.

'My trusty alarm clock wins again.'

'One day I will throw that thing in the Hot Zone.'

'You say that every day and it's still sitting there.' Daphne laughed at her antics as she finished pulling on a pair of jeans and moved onto the contamination suit that hung up at the front door.

The protective gear, which was made up of a combination of bin bags, tape, rubber gloves and a sealed face mask, was a normal part of life now. The suits that she and Poppy used were makeshift and had the scent of cheap rubber on them, far from the medical grade version they'd used during the pandemic or when the bombs first lit up the sky, but they had gifted those to two older citizens when they showed up in the hospital with no protective gear at all. At the time neither of the women were sure if anyone would survive this, but strong bodies likely had a better chance.

They could go without if it meant two more lives were saved.

Daphne shimmied her foot into the first leg carefully, working to keep the plastic intact until she could tape the two halves together in the centre. She pulled on her gloves and shoes before sliding the headgear on and looking towards Poppy as she started getting into her own suit.

'Do you want some help there, Pop?'

'Been putting this shit on for years now, I think I can do it myself.'

'Someone's a sour puss in the morning.'

They would eat with the rest of their community later. Daphne was so used to waiting that she barely noticed the hunger anymore.

Outside their apartment building, the young doctors were met with nothing but the quiet and the sight of people walking to their jobs at the end of the world. There was still snow on the ground, or maybe it was ash. No one could really tell the difference nowadays, not when you had to cover up in full body gear outside.

'Come on, slowpoke.'

The trudge to the hospital wasn't a long one but it gave them both the chance to witness the impact that the endless winter was having on their hometown. Everything was covered in the white substance and still particles of dust hung in the air like they were in a dimension of hell. Bodies of people who died on the street no longer piled up, the few who could handle it clearing them away. An attempt at reducing the already decayed atmosphere around them. They were the only saving grace in a world that had been thrown back into the dark ages.

Daphne lifted her head to look up at the eternally overcast sky, seeing the blackened clouds that shrouded their city and the whole world in an ice age that felt like it might never end. She knew it would, eventually, but she could be as old as some of her aging patients by the time the sun appeared again. It was a sombre thought but one that she couldn't shake, knowing the truth that so many wouldn't listen to when it was being repeated over the scientific radio stations while countries were throwing threats of nuclear action at each other over the oceans.

She had only listened to what she needed to do her job, the rest of it too depressing to mull over, but she saw the panicked expressions on the faces of people she treated back then. They were terrified down to their bones, and she couldn't blame them.

The hospital, a large white building in the middle of the town with too many windows and not enough beds, was one of the few survivors of the shockwave that the nearest bomb sent out. The benefit of having a new hospital built during the height of the pandemic and the constant threat of nuclear war – the structure had been reinforced to withstand a blast from fifty miles away. That was the best they could do under the circumstances, and they could only pray that a bomb wouldn't hit closer than that.

Unlike the pandemic wards of the past, folks had accepted everything that had happened, and the doomed community spirit was still palpable despite the knowledge that they were through the worst of it. Maybe it was the pure, unbridled hope that seemed to run through human veins no matter what, or perhaps it was just a delirium of spirit that was based in simple defeat, but everyone was happy.

Well, as happy as they could be, in the circumstances.

Daphne stripped out of her hazard suit at the door, red hair spilling out from beneath the plastic where her headgear didn't seal it against her skin. Then came the skin-tight rubber gloves to protect her from her patients' coughs. She got her stethoscope from her locker and entered into the main ward of the hospital. Her nostrils took in the fresh, clinically clean smell of antiseptic. For a moment, she almost felt like she was back in her old reality again, caring for patients suffering from things that she could cure, but that hadn't been the case for a long time.

'Daphne, bed eight, Nova symptoms. Doctor Nguyen - the *other* Doctor Nguyen - is looking for you in your office.' Kyle, one of the few internal medicine interns who had survived the first wave of the outbreak, handed Daphne a chart before leaving with Poppy to let her get on with her day unobstructed.

Bed eight was one of thirty-five that filled this cafeteria turned medical ward like sardines, and on it sat an old man waiting patiently for care while humming a rhythm under his breath that sounded suspiciously like an old country song that Daphne used to listen to on the drive to school with her mother.

'Mr. Zhao, my colleague tells me you're experiencing symptoms of Nova-25 today. Can you lean forward and let me listen to your breathing just now? Thank you, sir.' She smiled as she rested her hand on the man's shoulder to let him know where she was.

With her stethoscope on his back, she heard the characteristic rales of the virus in his left lung and then listened to the other side before allowing him to sit straight up again.

'How long have you had these symptoms, sir? Is there someone else in your family with the virus right now?'

'Please, call me Bohai, Mr. Zhao was my father. Only in recent weeks. I have been very lucky since I came here, no health problems, no illness, but I felt more pain in my chest this morning and thought it best to come in. I hear good things about your care from my neighbours, and they told me there were doctors who looked like me here.'

Daphne could hear the crackle in his voice. Her eyebrows furrowed together as she felt the glands in his neck for swelling too and found them engorged. She didn't show alarm, though. It was important to keep him calm.

'There are, sir. In fact, the woman in charge of this whole hospital is Vietnamese and she's the best doctor I know. Could you remove your shirt for me so I can check for any red areas of skin?'

When Bohai nodded, she stepped back, letting him unbutton his shirt until she could see the skin underneath. Though the redness wasn't a pronounced symptom in his case, there were a few patches growing on his chest, standing out against his pale, wrinkled skin. Checking his back, she used her fingers on his wrist to take his pulse rate manually.

'How did you lose your sight, Bohai? I didn't see any information about it on your chart.'

'Oh, the virus did not take my eyes. I was there when the bomb exploded over Glasgow. Not so close that I was vaporised, as you can see, but I looked into the light. It was instinct, I think, to look at the brightness, and it blinded me. But it was beautiful, my dear, like seeing God in person. So pure.'

Daphne felt comforted by the joyful expression on the old man's face. She rested her hand on his shoulder again and squeezed before writing down his heart rate. He talked about the great tragedy as if it were a spectacular artwork.

It was refreshing, and it relieved some of the ache she felt over the event.

'I've never met someone who witnessed one of the bombs before; you're very unique to have survived being so close. You can put your shirt back on now, sir.'

Bohai smiled and gripped her arm as a gesture of comradery. They knew each other's pain. It was the same pain the whole world felt.

'I do miss the old days. My childhood home, Wuzhen, it had many canals. They were so clear and perfect; I see them in my mind often. And the fish and chips, I miss the fish and chips from Glasgow. The good food of Scotland.' He laughed and Daphne did too, helping him when his hands shook on the last button of his shirt.

'I miss the fish and chips too, so much. Your condition hasn't progressed too far yet, Bohai, but I'm worried about your lungs getting worse in the cold temperatures so I'm going to admit you. The hospital is the warmest place you could be, trust me, we have very good insulation.' She smiled before waving to Iona, the nurse in charge of admission.

'Iona, this is Bohai. I'm admitting him to stay at the hospital to protect his lungs. I don't want him travelling home to get his things so if you can get him settled upstairs, I'll visit his home just now. Bohai, can you give me directions?'

'I can. It's...'

'Daphne, I need you over here!' She turned to find Kyle waving her over from across the room and sighed, fighting the urge to itch her nose before nodding, squeezing Bohai's hand to let him know she was still there.

'Always a fire to put out in my job! Give your directions to Iona just now, Bohai, she'll find someone else to get your things.' She smiled and he did too before Daphne moved quickly to the other bed when she heard coughing.

One of the two patients sitting on bed two couldn't have been more than ten years old and sounded like she was hacking up a lung with how hard she was coughing. Immediately, Daphne noticed the spots of blood on the tissue the girl had clutched against her mouth. In such a sterile environment like the hospital, she could smell it too. That metallic tang in the air.

'Okay, sweetheart, just lean forward and get it out. That's it, you're doing so good.' She snapped on a new pair of gloves before rubbing her back to comfort her, waiting until the coughing subsided before she helped lay the little girl back on the bed.

'That's it, my darling, just keep taking deep breaths. Can you tell me your name?'

'Allison.' She told her as Daphne placed her stethoscope on Allison's chest and listened.

The same rales that she had heard in Bohai's chest were there, but much more acute.

'Allison, nice to meet you. I'm Daphne. Sir, can you tell me about her symptoms? Are you her father?' She turned to the man on the end of the bed who looked so pale she was concerned he might keel over before Allison did.

'Yes, sorry. I'm Ruiraidh, I'm her uncle. She's been weak for a few months but recently, she started showing symptoms of Nova and coughing blood. We heard about the hospital from a family on our street, we live in Erskine.'

'You had a long journey, then. Okay, sir, we're going to get a culture of your niece's saliva to see what's going on inside. Coughing up blood is not a symptom of Nova-25 so I'm concerned something else is adding to her discomfort,' she said with a kind smile before looking down when Allison tapped her wrist, back to being a curious child rather than a suffering one now that she'd regained her breath.

'As for you, Miss Allison, there's a storybook session upstairs later with other kids in our community. We're reading Riley the River Otter today, have you read that one? Might be a bit young for you, I know.'

'I heard a boy outside talking about an asteroid earlier, that it's going to hit Earth. Is that true, Doctor Daphne?' Some blood from her previous coughing fit leaked from the side of Allison's mouth and Daphne wiped it away as she answered, the vague memory of her dream from the night before surfacing in her mind.

'I haven't heard anything about an asteroid heading for us today, darling, no. Besides, how would that boy know it was headed here? We can't see the sun, never mind space rocks!' she grinned, making Allison smile.

Still, the idea loomed in Daphne's head as she left the little girl and her uncle to rest and went in search of Poppy, finding her helping one of her amputee patients stand up from their bed.

'I'll see you again next week for a check-up, Mrs. Thomas, but please don't hesitate to come back in if something is wrong, as always.'

One of the abundant blessings of their ready-made nuclear war proof hospital was the stockpile of medical supplies packed into it, including materials for prosthetics that allowed Poppy to keep more people on their feet. Mrs Thomas was one of those patients, her lower leg having been taken by debris thrown out from the shockwave.

'Hey, Poppy, what did your brother want? Hi, Georgia.'

'Hi, dear. Thank you, Poppy.' The woman smiled at them both before taping the centre of her exposure suit and replacing her headgear and gloves, leaving through the exit of the hospital.

Poppy turned, disposing of her gloves while looking at Daphne.

'Nothing important, he just wanted to talk about a patient. Viola from Level 6 died during the night. What have you got?'

Daphne frowned at the news of Viola's death, shaking her head.

'Oh, Viola was so sweet. So far, I've had a kind old blind man who *saw* the Glasgow bomb explode, and a little girl who is coughing up blood, unrelated to Nova-25. I'm getting a culture done on her saliva.'

Poppy's interest piqued at the mention of Bohai.

'He *saw* the bomb? It took his sight?'

'Of course, it did. He looked directly into the light. He's okay otherwise, just some common Nova symptoms. I've admitted him to the hospital, so his lungs don't get any worse. Have you heard anything about this kid talking about an asteroid hitting us today? I'll tell you, misinformation still spreads like wildfire at the end of the world.' She sighed, running her hands through her hair while they were bare.

'Misinformation spreads around the planet worse than coronavirus did, I swear. How would the kid even know?'

'Exactly. Right, I'm going to scrub my hands and then start the reading session with the kids.'

102

Daphne remembered the good old days of scrubbing before going into a surgery. She never thought she'd missed the sterile smell of antiseptic and rubbing her skin raw when she was in the operating theatre more than twice a day. It was nauseating, how clean everything smelled, and now all she could do was hope the regular soap was enough to protect her patients.

Once she'd cleaned her hands as much as possible, she was finally able to take advantage of hanging out with the kids. They were so happy with what little they had nowadays, listening to her narrate one of the last children's books published and animate the characters with different voices.

Maybe in another life she could have been a voice actor. It was an amusing thought to have as she read.

'And then, a huge salty wave rose up and crashed into the coastline. It rushed and rushed towards Riley's river, rumbling through the ground to alert them to the threat, and soon all the otters in his colony were being swept into the sea, tumbling out of control. The water roared in Riley's ears like a lion, making him so dizzy he couldn't think, and then it stopped. Finally, the wave slowed, and Riley came to a stop in the vast ocean, out of place and…' Daphne brought herself to a stop, looking around as all the enraptured children moved their attention to Allison coughing.

'Allison, honey, take deep breaths.' Riley the River Otter was long forgotten as Daphne knelt on the ground with a collapsed Allison, blood leaking from her mouth.

Nothing presented this violently anymore. Nova followed her patients like a silent shadow, so Daphne rarely had to deal with immediate emergency treatment. People just died at home when their breathing finally failed them, but Allison was turning blue in front of her eyes, losing her ability to breathe, and all Daphne could do was start compressions when she lost her pulse.

'Daphne! Shit, Daph, there were cancerous cells in the blood of her saliva…' Kyle had been sitting in the circle of children watching her read, looking very out of place, but it meant he was close enough to help now.

'I don't give a shit about that right now! I lost her pulse, Kyle, I need a manual respirator!'

Kyle ran for the other side of the room, came back with the ambu-bag and started to give Allison air while Daphne continued to shove against her chest deep enough to keep her blood pumping. More blood leaked from her mouth with every compression as they spent over half an hour trying to get her back.

'Someone get me a goddamn intubation kit from upstairs!'

'Daphne, we don't have any intubation kits left. We lost them after the bomb casualties. We won't get her back, it's been too long…'

'She's just a little girl, Kyle!' She couldn't let her die.

'I know.'

Daphne finally stopped her hands from kneading Allison's chest, her bare skin spattered with droplets of the child's infected blood.

'You need to scrub your hands, Daph, she's infected.'

'This shouldn't have happened to her.'

'I know… Daphne!'

It felt like she was losing her first patient again, the same gut-wrenching, ripped out heart feeling filling her whole body head-to-toe as Daphne walked away from the tragedy. She had never lost a child before. Adults, sure, they died on her watch all the time. She'd been a surgeon long enough to lose more than a few people to her own mistakes, but never a child. It was a different kind of hopelessness than ran through her as she shut herself into the decontamination zone between the outside and the main ward.

Her whole body shook as she screamed in the enclosed space where no one would hear her, only an echo of her yell.

'Daphne? Can you open the door? I heard about Allison.'

'She's dead.'

'I know, and I'm sorry. Can you unlock the door, Daph?'

'I'm going outside for fresh air.'

'Remember your suit… Daphne!'

She already had the outer door open when Poppy's hand slammed against the glass in protest. It was fine, she'd come back in after a minute. She just needed to breathe first. The weather was the same as it had been that morning, only now she could feel that it was snowing. It wasn't ash, but the smell of decay and rot distracted her from that relief she felt. Everything was dead, even the trees, she just couldn't smell it with her mask on. The end of the world had been censored until now.

Without her exposure suit, she could feel the cold directly on her skin. It was bitter, angry with the people who had caused it. Daphne felt numb to that anger, her brain just running through all the ways she could have been better. The ways that would have helped her save Allison. The little girl who was too young and fragile to be killed by something that wasn't her fault. Her cancer was the fault of politicians who threw bombs at each other until those caught in the crossfire were annihilated by their stupidity.

Allison could have seen the sun come back with eyes young enough to appreciate it, skin fresh enough to feel its warmth. Now she was dead.

Daphne looked up at the sky with a pained groan, feeling the loss of Allison in her whole body as she dared to take her headgear off and take a breath. She just needed one breath of the outside, just one, until she noticed a light filtering through the black clouds.

Almost as if the sun was reappearing, but that wasn't possible yet, was it?

Collector of Memories

Ashleigh Tucker

I am the collector of memories,
I hold them close and out of sight.
Speak. Speak while I listen for centuries.

I hold the phantoms of families,
and the secrets they hold at night.
I am the collector of memories.

I hold the secrets of enemies,
you beg me to bring to light.
Speak. Speak while I listen for centuries.

I retrieve from the bodies,
after they have lost their fight
I am the collector of memories.

They share with me their stories,
so that I can share their plight.
Speak. Speak while I listen centuries.

There are no big ceremonies;
I would not know who to invite.
I am the collector of memories.
Speak. Speak while I listen for centuries.

Skinned

Ashleigh Tucker

Chapter 1

Harbour Seal pups swim with their mothers just hours after birth. They aren't born with that striking white coat that everyone imagines when thinking of a seal pup. Born with their adult pelage, they spend little time on the rocks or sandbanks before plunging into the sea, no matter how harsh or cold. Just miniature versions of their parents, their round heads can be seen from land, watching us while we watch them. They have every right to watch us. Our ancestors hunted them for their spotted skin, to keep us warm as it does them. However, a sealskin is of no use to a dead girl.

I look over the cliffside, down towards the shoreline noticing that there is not one officer down by the body. All four of them are gathered around the cars and vans. Two orange cones sit at the top of the steps, with three strips of blue and white police tape creating a barrier between the cones. *Useless.* I can see flocks of birds surrounding what I assume is our second victim. I zip up my coat fully, shoving my hands in my pockets before marching towards the officers.

'Can anyone tell me why the hell no one is down there stopping the gulls from eating the body?' I look around them all, demanding an answer.

A lanky officer with a buzzcut stumbles forward, nearly tripping over his own two feet. He extends a hand to me.

'Oh, hello. You must be Investigator DeJonge…'

He extends his hand, ignoring it I make eye contact.

'Well?' I ask, waiting for an answer.

'Oh, well, you see, we were waiting for you to arrive. We didn't want to go down and contaminate the scene.'

'So instead, for the,' I look at the watch on my wrist, 'half hour it took me to get here, you left the scene to be contaminated further by the local wildlife?'

If looks could kill, I'm sure all four of the officers would be on the floor. Dead. None of them even attempt to move. They all stand there, staring at me like rabbits in headlights. It takes all my strength not to lose my composure.

'Where's your Sergeant?'

'A fight broke out in town and one of our officers got injured, so she had to go deal with that.'

I throw my hands in the air and storm towards the steps. Standing behind the tape I can see why none of the officers are at the bottom of the cliff. There has to be at least three hundred steps or more. Made of large stones, they look like they will come loose with the slightest gust of wind, plummeting me down to the rocks below. Zigzagging back and forth, I can't see all the steps from the top of the cliff. *Bunch of lazy bastards.*

The wind batters my face, causing me to get a mouthful of hair. How I wish I brought my hat, or at least tied it back. It's going to be impossible to brush the knots out. Picking the strands of hair from my mouth I look at the four officers, walking around the pathetic barrier.

'Someone get your Sergeant on the phone and here NOW,' I call behind me.

Some steps are cracked, uneven and covered in moss. I can see that no one is following me; the lanky officer watches as I bounce down the steps, going as fast as I can. I glare up at the four men as they peer down at me. My foot slips.

I land on grass at the side of the steps, my hand stopping me from rolling down the rest of the cliffside. Taking a deep breath, I try to calm myself. Lying on the ground I look up at the officers.

'What use are you all just standing there? Get down these steps and do your job!'

Reluctantly, two of the officers start their slow descent, when I am already halfway down. I get up, wiping mud on my black jeans, before continuing to hobble down the stairs. I'm surprised the public can use this death-trap of a stairway; there's no handrail, it's dangerous and that's without considering the bone-breaking rocks at the bottom. How did someone manage to get a body down these steps? Or force a hostage down them?

By the time I reach the bottom, I can feel the salt sticking to my skin. The wind isn't as assaulting as it was on the way down. Watching where I stand, I stumble across the rockpools, towards the flocking birds. There are a couple of large black ravens amongst the gulls, fighting for their pound of flesh.

'Get! Get!' I wave my arms around, shouting to frighten the birds.

It has the opposite effect. The seagulls begin to dive at me, squawking as they refuse to give up their meal. I notice a raven hopping across the pools, with what appears to be long yellow strands of straw in its mouth. I eventually make it to the body and the birds continue to attack, but I manage to get them off the corpse. The two officers finally reach the bottom, deterring the birds mobbing me. I guess they were willing to fight me alone for the meat, but not three people. They perch on the cliffside, fighting over what little bits of flesh they managed to escape with.

With the scavengers gone I finally get a good look at the body and realisation hits me. My stomach clenches. The raven isn't carrying straw. It had a bit of scalp, hair still attached. I can't decide what I hate more, the gulls or the ravens. She's been fed upon by the seagulls, but the ravens have taken her eyes. Empty sockets stare up at me, reminding me of a lamb after a raven plucks out its eyeballs. For a second, the black holes distract me from the rest of her…but only for a second.

This body is just as gruesome as the first one found. Flies swarm, just as eager as the birds, crawling all over the grey spotted flesh that has crudely been sewn onto the woman's arms and legs. This corpse has more skin than the first; one of her arms is nearly covered, and as I get closer the scent of spoiled meat assaults me. It's not the victim that smells, it's the rotting seal skin. Unlike the first victim, Eve

Manson, this girl was alive when the killer sewed the skin onto her. Eve was dead, drowned in the sea before someone mutilated her body. I know this second victim was alive because each messy stitch used to attach the flesh bled. A dead body doesn't bleed.

Eve Manson was just twenty-three when she was murdered. With beautiful auburn hair and delicate features she reminded me of my daughter Elise, my youngest daughter, and the double of me in my youth. Elise was just nineteen when she, and her cousin Tracy, went missing. They went out for a night of drinking with friends but never made it to the bar. It's been six years since. There's been no sign of the girls, and despite my efforts, the case went cold quickly. The only evidence is a picture of a white van that I eventually found burnt to a crisp in an abandoned car park.

I was wrong, I do know what I hate more. It's not the gulls or the ravens. It's someone I have never met before, never seen. The one who has tortured two young women, killing both in the process. For the sake of these girls and their families, I will find this monster.

I put on a pair of latex gloves and lift a flap of seal skin on her arm; it's not properly attached. The human skin underneath has been peeled away, exposing muscle, leaving fresh flesh against rotting. Maggots crawl, festering in the wounds, letting off their own putrid stench. I hear the sound of retching behind me and look over my shoulder to see the lanky officer, covering his mouth.

'If you're going to be sick, do it as far from the body as you can.' I point towards the steps, where the other two officers are standing and notice a woman officer walking towards us.

'Investigator DeJonge, I'm Sergeant Morris. Sorry I was not here to greet you but there's been an incident.'

'Forgive me if I don't shake your hand,' I hold my gloved hands up, 'don't think you would appreciate it.'

The blonde woman nods, looking at the body, then out to sea. It's a gorgeous sight. There's nothing for hundreds of miles, just ocean and horizon. The sky is so clear you can barely tell where it starts and where the water ends. Not a cloud to be seen. If it wasn't for the wind,

I would think I was in Spain. Maybe even consider sunbathing. If only I didn't turn out like a boiled lobster whenever the sun is out.

'So, do we know who this girl is?' I stand up, taking my gloves off.

'We haven't confirmed it with DNA or prints yet, but it's a small town. I'm confident that's Mia Gunn. She's something of a star in the community. Fastest swimmer we have ever seen, her times were Olympic standard. She qualified to swim at the trials next week.'

'We will have to get her ID confirmed. Who found her?' I shove the gloves into my pocket.

'Fiona Harold. She came down here to take pictures of her dog, thought the body was a seal or sheep that fell down the cliff. She only checked what it was because the dog refused to leave it alone. She was a state when Officer Banks arrived.' She points to the incompetent officer beside her.

'She couldn't stop crying, telling me it was Mia Gunn.' Banks adds.

'I'll need to interview Ms Harold. Are there any family members we can contact? Mum or dad? I would prefer to ID her through DNA, no need to let her family see her like this.'

'Her parents are part of the religious nutjobs,' Banks answers, causing Morris to glare at him.

'Excuse me?' I lock eyes with him.

'Oh sorry, um… I mean…' He shrinks a little, looking between me and Morris.

'Banks, go. Phone the fire brigade we will need them to help move the body.' Morris covers her eyes, shaking her head.

'Yes. Yes, I'll go do that, thanks. Sorry.' He scurries away, nearly tripping over his own two feet.

How he became an officer is beyond me, he doesn't have the confidence or demeanour for it. He's skittish and doesn't seem to deal well with confrontation. Banks may be fine for a small town, but he'd be eaten alive in a city. I suspect he isn't taken seriously by his colleagues, let alone by the public. Nothing about him demands

111

respect. Unlike Sergeant Morris, whose strong straight stance screams that she's a leader.

'Religious nutjobs?' I look at Morris and she shakes her head again.

'I'm sorry about him, but I can't say I have a different opinion. He was talking about a religious group called *The Disciples of God.* They're just a stone's throw away from being a cult. They've been in the town for nearly thirteen years and have bought up all the land they can. They have a little over 600 members now, give or take.'

'A cult? In the Scottish Highlands?'

Well, this is something I've never experienced before. Sure, there are groups throughout Scotland. *The Jehovah's Witnesses, Free Masons, Children of God,* and a few others. But I've never heard of *The Disciples of God.*

'The group started in America and then expanded into Scotland. They aren't a registered religious group, so I'd class them as a cult,' Morris says, her lips forming a tight line.

'So, Mia and her parents were part of this group?'

'Mia left the compound as soon as she was able to; she wanted to pursue swimming for the Olympics. Her parents are still in it, pretty much disowned her when she left. Poor girl. She got a restraining order against the group's "leader" Raymond Owens, claiming he was harassing her, demanding she re-joins the group.'

'I guess her parents wouldn't be able to tell us if she was missing then. Why didn't she leave town? Start fresh?' I use my hand to shield my eyes from the sun; it seems to be getting stronger with every passing minute.

'She couldn't afford to leave the town, so she said. She works at a little café on the street, I only ever see her working or on her way to the pool. Never went out and didn't have many friends. I think she stayed because of her younger siblings, two girls and three boys. She was constantly advocating trying to get custody of the girls.'

'Well, there's a motive.' I unzip my jacket, pulling out a notebook and pen from an inside pocket. 'What about the boys? Was she not trying to get custody of them?'

'Two of the boys are adults. Thomas- Mia's twin- is twenty-one, while Liam's nineteen. She did try to get custody of the eight-year-old, Michael, but she was desperate to get the girls.'

I begin to write the details Morris is sharing down. Names, ages, and facts. I will have to confirm all the information given as the investigation goes on. From what I'm hearing this group, *The Disciples of God*, have a good motive to want Mia gone. She refused to return to the group and was actively trying to get custody of her siblings. Attention any cult would not appreciate. Not to mention her restraining order against their leader.

'What's your take on the situation? Do you think the group would kill someone?'

'If I'm honest, I don't think there's much they wouldn't do. It's just a case of getting the evidence to prove it.'

'Well, I think this group is a good place to start looking. Will one of your officers be able to take me to Mia's parents' home, or somewhere I can find them?' I look over my shoulder towards two officers. I'm doubtful they would be able to complete the simple task of showing me to an address. I don't think they could even write it down correctly if I were to ask. I'd place money on them not being able to give me the address for their own precinct. One officer hits the other one in the privates, laughing as his partner doubles over. Just a bunch of glorified schoolboys playing dress up.

'I can get one of them to take you, but you won't need to go far.' Morris points behind me. That field there belongs to Owens, and all the fields behind it for a good nine miles or so.'

'So, this harbour belongs to him?' I ask and Morris shakes her head.

'No. This,' she says, turning and pointing towards the steps, 'is public property. He tried to buy it, but the council wouldn't sell. It's a popular area for tourists throughout the summer. It would have been no use to Owens, he only wanted it because he's greedy.'

I write down this information before closing my notebook and putting it back in my coat pocket. So, *The Disciples of God* own the land at the top of where an ex-member of their cult is found dead. A member that had custody battles and restraining orders with members of this group. I wonder if there's any connections between Eve and this group. I'll have to speak to her parents. Find out if there are any ties between them and *The Disciples*. Right now, they are my main suspects.

I look up at the top of the steps, seeing the fire engine pull up. My phone vibrates in my pocket, and I check it. It's a message from the medical examiner.

'The medical examiner will be here in five minutes. So don't let them move the body until he arrives. Anything he wants or needs he gets,' I tell Morris and she nods.

I take one last look around the scene. The raven is still sitting on the cliff, pulling at the piece of scalp it got away with. The examiner may want that piece back, so good luck to the officer that has to retrieve it. All the birds are perched, waiting for their chance to resume their meal. I walk to the edge of the rockpools; the water is calm. Gentle waves hit the rocks and I look out at the water. There's a dark head bobbing on top, watching me. Then a second and a third appear, closer to the rocks. Seals are curious creatures. I could stand here for hours, and they would continue to watch me.

If they knew that one of their family members has been skinned, they wouldn't be as enthusiastic to stay. Knowing that they are at risk of being hunted by this same killer, they'd stay out at sea. Away from the cruel actions of humans. I watch the three seals, slowly drifting to the shore. One so close I can see its large circular eyes look into my own.

Maybe they do know.

A note from the author:

My inspiration for *Seaweed and Roses* came from my ongoing journey of learning to accept and love myself and my illness. Diagnosed with Cystic Fibrosis at 10 years old, I have struggled dealing with my medications, physio, and mental health. Now, with the development of drugs such as Kaftrio, I know I have to come to terms with my illness. Instead of using writing as a way to escape my life I am using my writing abilities to explore my complicated feelings about my illness. My other two pieces were inspired by the BA(Hons) course. Before our *Crime Pays* module, I said, 'I don't write or read crime' and wanted to write a crime opening that appealed to readers that don't like/read crime. I have never seen myself as a crime writer but in less than a year I have two novel openings that I think are very 'Tartan Noir'.

Ashleigh Tucker studied Creative Writing BA (Hons) at the University of the Highlands and Islands graduating in 2023. She is currently unpublished but is working on two Scottish crime novels: Skinned *and* Salted Creel. *Currently she has been accepted into an internship at Ringwood Publishing. She has a website: http://ashleightucker875247601.com; Instagram: @ash_tuc; TikTok: @ashleight607. In addition to these social medias Tucker has also started a TikTok: @aff.a.daunder, and Instagram: @aff_a_daunder, where she explores the beauty of the Scottish Highlands while looking for writing inspiration.*

The Wizard's Daughters

Charlotte Usher

CUT TO:

EXT: THUNDERTON HOUSE, ELGIN -- AFTER MIDNIGHT -- NOVEMBER 2019.

Thunderton House is boarded up. Work is in progress on the outside of the building. There is a street light.

ALLEGRA (30s) is an engineer from Padua in Italy. She's dressed in dark clothing with a hood obscuring her face. An expensive, antique silver pentacle shines against her dark clothing. She has a small backpack. She's wearing a headlight. She uses a crowbar she has brought with her to remove one of the boards to the windows. She climbs in and replaces the board from the inside.

CUT TO:

INT: EMPTY ROOM ON FIRST FLOOR OF THUNDERTON HOUSE, ELGIN -- SAME NIGHT, AFTER MIDNIGHT -- NOVEMBER 2019

ALLEGRA investigates the wood paneled room. It's bare except for an upended chair but the cornicing and fireplace hint at former grandeur. She touches the walls and the fireplace.

> ALLEGRA
>
> Ciao. I'm here.

Allegra draws a pentacle in chalk on the floor and positions candles around the five points. She switches off her headlight and lights the first candle with a lighter. She lights each one.

> ALLEGRA
>
> (in Latin)
>
> I'm the Wizard's child.

> She picks up the chair and places it in the centre of the pentacle.

INT: FIRST FLOOR ROOM, THUNDERTON HOUSE, ELGIN – MOMENTS LATER – NOVEMBER 2019

From her backpack ALLEGRA removes a large, LEATHERBOUND BOOK.

Allegra opens the book and inside the front cover there's a handwritten family tree. The handwriting is beautiful. It starts with Robert Gordon III and Margaret Frigg – unmarried. There is a dotted line to their daughter Robina Frigg, The Bastard. Allegra touches Robina's name.

> AllEGRA
>
> (in Latin)
>
> Show me.
>
> ALLEGRA sniffs.
>
> ALLEGRA
>
> Smells like a peat fire.

FADE TO:

INT: BEDROOM ON FIRST FLOOR of THUNDERTON HOUSE, ELGIN -- NIGHT -- November 1704.

From the book in ALLEGRA'S hands a scene appears:

The bedroom is Queen Anne era elegant. There's a fire in the fireplace. There's a four-poster bed with curtains. Either side of the fireplace are two Queen Anne style chairs and there's a table with food and wine on it. A big black dog sleeps on the rug in front of the fire. Somewhere in the room is a writing desk.

SIR ROBERT GORDON III (57) is sitting in one of the chairs. He's dressed in clothes typical of a country gentleman of the era who has returned from a ride. His sword, hat and cloak are near the door to the room. He's reading Isaac Newton's Optick, but his gaze keeps moving to the bed.

ROBINA FRIGG (14) is lying asleep in the bed. She looks like she's had a really good scrub and is wearing a white shift.

Allegra fades into the background. She's still in modern dress. Sir Robert and Robina don't acknowledge her presence.

Robina wakes up. She appears frightened.

> SIR ROBERT
>
> Hungry? Calm yourself, wench.
> I am not going to eat you.

Robina pulls the covers up to her neck and stares at him.

Sir Robert takes a robe from a hook and flings it on the bed.

> SIR ROBERT
>
> Put it on. I will turn my back.
>
> ROBINA
>
> Fit ye gonna do ta me?

SIR ROBERT

Of all the crimes I am accused
of, defiling my own cubs is not
one of them. You look so like
my dear Lizzie that I cannot
deny your whoring mother told
the truth of that.

Sir Robert turns to face the fireplace. He
makes a grand sweeping gesture of it.

Robina dresses in the robe and then picks up a
heavy vase.

When Sir Robert turns round he grins at her.

SIR ROBERT

You have a great deal of pluck
to face your Lord armed. Put it
down.

ROBINA

The gossips say I killed my
whoring mither. Fit makes you
think I would nae kill the
father that's a stranger t' mi?

Sir Robert is amused.

SIR ROBERT

You've saved my life once
today.

ROBINA

Your illwillie bastard of a
coachman threatened tae whip
me. It's just you and me noo
and your sword's o'er there.

SIR ROBERT

That vase cost our hosts a
pretty penny. Neither of us can
afford to be evicted. Are you
responsible for your mother's
demise?

Robina shakes her head.

ROBINA

A fisher right off his boatie
walked all the way fae Seatown.
When my mither telt him she was
on her bleed, he didnae like
it. Hit her wi' his stick then
fled. The villagers said I
must be a whore like my mither
and a witch like you. I wis
running awa' when I saw you in
trouble at the loch.

Robina places the vase down gently and steps
away from it like she's worried she will break
it.

Sir Robert pours her a glass of wine and hands
it to her.

SIR ROBERT

You must be sharp-set. Eat.

ROBINA

I'm used to nae eating.

Robina sits in the chair that Sir Robert
indicates. She sniffs at the wine.

SIR ROBERT

What did your mother name you?

            ROBINA

    Robina. After my father.

    SIR ROBERT

    You don't quite speak like one
    of my peasants. A bit rough but
    I can understand you without a
    translator.

    ROBINA

    I telt the minister if he did
    nae teach me to read and write,
    I'd tell at the kirk what I
    heard him do wi' my mither. I
    read a little in Latin and
    English.

Sir Robert reaches down beside the chair and
picks up a grubby sack with books in it.

Robina moves forward.

            ROBINA

    That's mine.

Sir Robert removes the three books: *The Bride-
Woman Counselor by Rev Chudleigh, The Blazing
World by Margaret Cavendish and a King James
Bible*. He also removes scraps of parchment, ink
and quills.

            SIR ROBERT

            Interesting. This belongs
            to my library. How did you
            get it?

He indicates The Blazing World.

ROBINA

The steward. He visits my mither ti diddle. Have nae read it yet.

SIR ROBERT

Is there any man in Duffus you haven't blackmailed?

ROBINA

The Bishop wanted the minister tae come down on the sinners of the parish. They didnae want to get caught. The Bishop gave me that… so I didnae tell them about fit he got up tae wi' mi' mither.

Robina points to the Bride-Counsellor by Rev Chudleigh.

Sir Robert picks up the book.

SIR ROBERT

If you've read this appalling description of womanhood you ought to have the Ladies Defence as well. My Lizzie helped me with my experiments. A brilliant scientific mind like she had or that of Margaret Cavendish should not be crippled because of gender.

Now what do I do with you? You know too much and I can't have you telling people of my plans to disappear.

ROBINA

I won't tell. Won't your family
be worried?

SIR ROBERT

My son is of an age he wishes
to be the laird

My wife has a new love. We've
not been getting

along so well since our
daughter died. She's going

to hold a funeral. She knows my
plans.

ROBINA

Who will believe the daughter
of the parish whore o'er

Lady Elizabeth? If I go back to
Duffus they will kill

me for my mither's murder.

SIR ROBERT

I don't think I can risk
letting you escape but nor can
I harm you. I'm getting on in
age and want to continue my
academic pursuits without the
local pitchfork mob screaming
witchcraft every time it goes
bang. Nobody must know I'm
still alive.

SFX: There's a banging within the building.
Someone running up the stairs.

Sir Robert and Robina don't acknowledge the bang and continue interacting in the

background.

A spotlight falls on ALLEGRA who closes the LEATHERBOUND BOOK.

Allegra closes the book and Sir Robert; Robina and the rest of 1704 vanishes. She stands up and places the book on the chair. The candles go out.

CUT TO:

INT: BEDROOM ON FIRST FLOOR OF THUNDERTON HOUSE, ELGIN -- NIGHT -- moments later, NOVEMBER 2019.

The candles have gone out.

ALLEGRA has turned her headlight back on. She takes a heavy metal bar from her backpack and faces the door, prepared to attack.

STEVE INNES (30s) a police officer enters. He's wearing full uniform.

> STEVE
>
> For God's Sake. Put that down. We've had a report of a break in. When I heard where it was, I thought it might be you -- Again!

> Allegra puts the metal bar down.

> ALLEGRA
>
> I have to do this. I told you about that when we met at the Michael Kirk. Policeman or no,

> I will not let you interfere
> with the process.

          STEVE

> When I decided to let you off
> with a warning you mean?

> (beat)

> I'll do you a deal?

Steve checks his watch.

          STEVE

> I get off duty in half an hour.
> Have a coffee with me, and I'll
> pretend   I   didn't   find
> anything.

          ALLEGRA

> It's two am. Nowhere in this
> god forsaken backward place is
> open.

          STEVE

> It'll have to be McDonalds. Do
> we have a deal?

          ALLEGRA

> Have you got a car?

          STEVE

> Yep.

          ALLEGRA

> Take me up to Birnie Kirk and
> you have a deal. I will go for
> a coffee with you after I have
> finished my quest.

STEVE

The deal was I wouldn't arrest
you. Not that I would help you
in this mad obsession of yours.

ALLEGRA

I promised my grandmother I'd
take her to visit the place her
family began. She was so fit
and healthy, we thought we had
plenty of time. Then she died
when the bridge collapsed
without us coming here to do
this together… well... I had to
come alone.

STEVE

Fuck, Allegra. Your story
entangles me more every time we
meet. There has to be a better
way than breaking into every
building in that damn book.

ALLEGRA

I wrote letters to the owners
but they didn't get back to me
in time. If I don't do it this
month, I have to wait a year.
Sir Robert staged the final
scene in the churchyard. Where
he cheated on his deal with the
devil by dying on consecrated
ground. No need to break in
this time.

STEVE

That bit of the story I know.

ALLEGRA

According to Robina, he'd left
his valuables with the
minister who was his friend. He
was spotted and staged the
accident.

Steve checks his watch.

STEVE

I gather the body didn't
disappear or the horse get
eaten by hell hounds?

ALLEGRA

The witness ran home
terrified. That's what the
minister, Sir Robert's friend,
told everyone had happened.

Allegra takes a smartphone out of her back
pocket and checks the time.

ALLEGRA

Give me forty-five minutes.
I'll meet you outside TK Maxx.

Steve leaves.

Allegra relights the candles and turns off her
headlight. She sits on the chair and opens the
LEATHERBOUND BOOK. She fades into the
background.

FADE TO:

**INT: BEDROOM ON FIRST FLOOR OF THUNDERTON
HOUSE, ELGIN -- NIGHT -- MOMENTS LATER,
NOVEMBER 1704.**

SIR ROBERT and ROBINA are both stood up by the fireplace.

Sir Robert attaches his sword and dresses in his hat, cloak and boots as he speaks.

> SIR ROBERT
>
> It is settled, my child. You will come to Italy with me as my daughter and assistant. I need to retrieve my valuables from a friend. Rest now.

Sir Robert leaves the room with a sweep. The dog that has been sleeping by the fireplace follows him out.

Robina sits at the writing desk. *The Story of Robina Frigg, Bastard Daughter of the Wizard.* It's the same handwriting as the Family Tree at the start is written in.

Allegra closes the leatherbound book. She blows out four of the five candles.

Robina blows out the candle on her desk and the same time Allegra blows out the fifth candle. The room his dark.

SFX: Allegra closing the door on her way out.

CUT TO:

EXT: Outside tk.maxx (opposite the thunderton), Elgin -- about 3am -- NOVEMBER 2019

ALLEGRA is waiting. She's playing a game on her phone.

STEVE appears from the direction of the police station with two reusable coffee mugs and a lunchbox. He hands Allegra a mug and opens the lunchbox.

STEVE

As we're not going to McDonald's I thought I'd introduce to a good Scottish pie. You have the choice between macaroni cheese or beans and mash?

Allegra smiles at him. She takes the beans and mash pie.

ALLEGRA

Both look equally revolting, but I'm hungry. Let's go finish this part of their story.

STEVE

As long as we clean up the funky gubbins afterwards. I already have one Church of Scotland minister complaining about the desecration of his chapel.

They walk up the pedestrianised bit back the way Steve arrived. As they walk they eat their pies and have an indistinct but animated conversation.

SFX: A horse riding past them.

SIR ROBERT (V.O)

'Oh wha hasna heard o' that man of renown

The Wizard, Sir Robert of Gordonstoun?

The wisest o' warlocks.The Morayshire Cheil

```
The despot o' Duffus and friend o'
the de'il'
```

FADE TO BLACK.

THE END

A note from the author:

In 2015 I won a place on The BBC Room to Write, a BBC Scotland comedy forum. It was the first time I had ever written a script and it beat out 3000 other scripts to win the place. Unfortunately, a mix of imposter syndrome, not sharing a sense of humour with the producers and my own inexperience meant I didn't get the most out of my time with the BBC. It did result in a short monologue being produced which gave me a production credit but I struggled to plot out a longer script. I finished what should have been a life changing experience despondent, blocked and unsure where to go next.

In 2019 I started the BA in Creative Writing in the Highlands and Islands with UHI. The course has helped me identify the deeper issues with my writing such as how my North of England voice was at odds with the fact I had lived in Moray for most of my life. This piece was the first piece I wrote where I felt the script flowed and where I combined my writing voice with the location that had become my home.

Postscript

Dr. Sara Bailey

Reading through this anthology filled me with so many emotions. The pieces made me cry, laugh, and gasp in delight but most of all, they made me feel proud.

I developed this degree along with the team in 2017, and we launched our first-year group in 2018. Our intention was to fill a gap in the Highlands & Islands. While there were several MA programmes, there was not a Single Honours undergraduate degree in Creative Writing at that time.

The vision was to create a space where students could explore a variety of different genres, writing styles and techniques whilst at the same time learning about the business of writing. I wanted them to have four years of exploration and find things out about themselves and their abilities that they'd not thought to look for previously.

I strongly believe we all know how to tell a story, that it is deeply ingrained in us all. This degree, to an extent, is about teaching us to get out of our own way and let that story come through in whatever form it chooses. This anthology is a demonstration of that belief. I wish I had space to talk about each of piece and how they all touched me. But suffice to say, they all did.

Handing over the degree to Kirstie Gunn was a wrench, but a degree needs to grow and evolve, and after four years at the helm, it was time for fresh eyes and perspectives. Looking at what Kirstie and the students have achieved with this anthology makes me see what a wise decision that was.

I have absolutely no doubts at all we will all be hearing from these students in the future. I am so excited to see what they do next.

Printed in Great Britain
by Amazon

32286366R00079